FUSED

Claremore, OK

For the art of storytelling and the power of a group coming together to accomplish a goal

Foreword

These stories are works of fiction. All names, characters, institutions, places, and events portrayed in each story are either products of the author's imagination or are used fictitiously. Any resemblance to actual persons, living or dead, business establishments, or events is entirely coincidental.

CONTENTS

ACKNOWLEDGMENTS

Special thanks to Debbie and Alger at Northeast Technology Center

1. THE GAMES II

By JOHN D KETCHER JR

The Liberal Nationalist Party had taken over and declared all other parties illegal and the leadership of those parties arrested. Hand-picked loyalists from the DNC replaced them. The bloodless coup was over in 24 hours with the help of the National Guard and local law enforcement. All elected officials, local, state and federal, were arrested and jailed until their usefulness could be determined. Their value determined by their answers at the Games.

The first game held two months ago ended in the death of the district commander and fourteen security personnel who were attacked by six lions. One prisoner, Pastor Eagle, was held responsible for the death of District Commander Terry McVile and taken to the county jail.

***

Present Day

Pastor Eagle knelt by his bed and prayed. He prayed for his jailers, enemies, family, friends and lastly for his nation.

1

Since District Commander Terry McVile's untimely death, Pastor Eagle has been in solitary confinement. His daily routine consisted of sleeping, eating and praying. More of the latter than the former. He was not allowed any contact except for the guards who brought his meals.

The door lock clicked open, but the guard hesitated before going into Pastor Eagle's cell. Deputy Johnston dreaded this part of his job. Eagle spooked him, as well as the other deputies, to no end. He greeted each deputy by name without looking at them and asked how their families are doing. The real scary part is he knew the names of all the wives and children. *How did he know their names?* Finally, Deputy Johnston entered and placed the dinner tray at the foot of the prisoner's bed.

"Good evening, Deputy Johnston," Eagle said, continuing to pray with closed eyes.

"How's Carol, Daniel, and little Jessica this evening?"

Silence.

"What's on the menu?"

No response.

"Thank you, Deputy Johnston and God bless you."

Deputy Johnston exited the cell without saying a word. His body trembled once outside. *How does he know it's me?* Johnston thought to himself, *it's unnerving the way he knows the name of each deputy bringing his meal without even looking at them. Eagle gives me the creeps. I don't care if he's a famous political prisoner, I'm putting in for a transfer back to patrol.*

Eagle placed the tray on his knees and prayed for his meal. "Dear Heavenly Father. I give thanks for your mercy and goodness. Bless this food for the nourishment of my body. Bless my jailers and forgive them their trespasses. In the Precious Name of Jesus. Amen."

Removing the cover, he placed the stale bread on top of his pillow for later. Eagle picked the raw potato and ate his evening meal. Finishing, he returned the tray to the foot of his bed. Looking at the camera, he smiled.

"Tower to Johnston. The prisoner has finished his supper."

Standing outside Eagle's cell door, Deputy Johnston forced himself to open the door and retrieve the prisoner's tray.

"That was a fine meal. My compliments to the chef."

Still no response.

"Until next time. Good night and God bless you, Deputy Johnston."

The cell door closed behind the deputy.

***

Deputy Larry Green was in the control tower monitoring the bank of computer screens, watching the prisoners confined in the four cell blocks when three men walked into the room. He recognized the shift supervisor, Deputy Dan Block, and Security Chief Gabriel Walker. *The third man must be the new District Commander of Northeastern Oklahoma, James Keller,* Green thought.

"We have four cell blocks," Deputy Block said. "Block A is for non-violent prisoners; Block B for prisoners in solitary confinement; Block C houses the female population; and Block D holds the more violent offenders. Up here in the control tower, we have a deputy on duty for 12-hour shifts. This evening Deputy Green is monitoring all four blocks and controls all access to the doors within the building."

"We're here to check on the prisoner in solitary confinement. Can you bring him up on your monitor?" James Keller asked.

"We can now. Before Eagle's arrival, we did not have

cameras inside the sleeping areas. Deputy bring up the prisoner in Block B."

Deputy Green rolled his swivel chair down the bank of screens and punched several buttons, bringing up the cell Pastor Eagle was housed onto a larger screen.

"What's the prisoner doing?" asked the district commander.

"He's praying. That's his daily routine: sleep, pray and eat. When I'm on duty, that's all the prisoner does. He sleeps maybe four hours a night and a one hour nap in the afternoon, but the rest of the time he's kneeling by his bed praying."

"What's he saying? Are you able to record what he says?"

"The recording device came with the new camera. Let me turn up the volume."

"…and Heavenly Father, I pray for those four men in the control tower who are watching me as I praise your name. Fill them with Your Love and Mercy. Show them the error of their ways, especially the new district commander, James Keller. Amen." Pastor Eagle paused a moment, then investigated the camera and smiled. Turning away, he continued praying.

"Turn the volume off," the district commander hollered. "How did he know I was up here? Who told him my name?"

"No one has spoken to him since he was brought here two months ago. The guards are spooked because he calls them by name without looking at them. We've had a high rate of turn-over in jailers since this prisoner has been here," Deputy Block answered.

"Bring the prisoner to your office," Keller said. "I want to talk to him."

"Yes, Sir," Deputy Block answered. "Deputy Green, have Johnston escort the prisoner to my office."

4

"Deputy Johnston bring…"

**

"Do you know why you are here?" The district commander asked.

"Because you people blame me for the death of District Commander McVile," Eagle replied.

"Why did she die?"

"She didn't heed the advice of Security Chief Walker."

Keller looked directly at Walker and said: "What advice did you give her?"

Walker thought about that night when the lions ripped Terri McVile apart. *We were standing at the gate. I told her to wait. Why didn't she heed my advice to wait outside the gate? Why did she hate Eagle so much to disregard her safety?*

"I advised her to wait outside the security fence until we secured Mr. Eagle," Walker answered, all the while wondering how Eagle knew about the conversation between him and McVile.

"Why didn't she heed your advice?"

"That's something only she could answer, but I believe it had to do with her hatred for Mr. Eagle. The two had a run-in last year," Said a worried Walker, hoping for this conversation to end before the new district commander asked why he was the only one to survive.

Looking back at Eagle the district commander asked: "What was the run-in about?"

"We had different religious views, Herr Keller." Came the reply.

"Why did you call me Herr?" Keller asked as he leaned forward.

"Because you and Fraulein McVile share the same beliefs."

"I believe you referred her to a goose-stepping moron. Isn't that right Mr. Eagle?"

"Yes, Herr Keller"

"And would you call me a goose-stepping moron?"

"You're wearing the same brown uniform. Your political party is executing Christians, political prisoners, and those who disagree with your party's ideology. That's what Nazi Germany did to the Jews, political prisoners, and dissidents during World War II." Eagle then leaned forward and stared Keller straight in the eyes, "I was there in Germany helping liberate those prisoners who, by the grace of God, survived the death camps. Those people living in Nazi Germany and later occupied countries lived in fear of the brown shirts, later known as the Gestapo. Today Americans are living in fear of those brown shirts. Those who do not know history are doomed to repeat history. So yes, Herr Keller, you are a goose-stepping moron." Pastor Eagle answered.

Keller pounded the desk with both fists yelling "Shut up, damn you. You know nothing. We have united this country under one rule, one ideology. We have brought peace to everyone. It's people like you who divided this nation. All you had to do was accept our ideology, and you could have lived in peace." He screamed.

"A false peace is what you have to offer, Herr Keller. The same false peace Hitler offered to the people of the countries he conquered." Eagle replied. "Your peace is a limited peace and only as long as people obey your rules and keep their mouths shut. Otherwise, they would be in jail with me. Isn't that right, Herr Keller?"

A red-faced district commander leaned across the desk and said through gritted teeth, "While you're here, you are not to pray. Prayer is forbidden. Do you understand?"

"Or what Herr Keller? I'm scheduled for execution

soon. What more can you do to me?" Eagle turned and looked directly at Chief Walker with piercing eyes.

"Get him out of here!" Keller screamed. "Take him back to his cell, now."

"Now you're beginning to sound like Fraulein McVile. I'll be praying for you." Pastor Eagle said as Deputy Johnston shoved him out of the office.

***

"Chief Walker, I won't be needing you anymore this evening. Let the driver know I have several more places to go."

"Aye, sir. What time would you like us to pick you up in the morning?"

"8 a.m. will be fine. We'll have breakfast at that café on the east side of town. What was its name?"

"Eastside Café, sir," Walker replied.

"And why do they call it Eastside Café?" Keller asked.

"Because it's on the east side of town," Said Walker.

"Interesting. Until tomorrow."

***

Arriving home behind the Salina Police Station, Walker hung his gun belt in the hall closet and headed to the kitchen. He found his wife of two years straightening up the kitchen. Leaning against the kitchen door frame, he reflected on his life with her, and how lucky he was to have married such a beautiful woman. Naomi was a tall, slender dark-haired, full blood Cherokee. Always the optimist. She turned and smiled at him.

"Sorry, I'm late getting home. It's been one heck of a day. The new district commander arrived, and I was busy with him all day long. I haven't had a chance to eat. What do we have?" Gabriel asked.

"I'll heat the pot roast I cooked earlier," Naomi said "Were you and the district commander with that prisoner today? How is that prisoner doing?"

"Mr. Eagle? Well, he sure upset the new district commander a little while ago," Gabriel said as he sat down at the kitchen table.

"How so?"

"Mr. Eagle called him a goose-stepping moron for starters. I've never seen anyone get so red-faced angry as the district commander. It looked like his head was going to pop wide open," Gabriel said as he leaned over and put his head in his hands. "There was a moment when the district commander asked me why the former commander didn't heed my warning."

"What were you worried about?" Naomi said as she heard the fear in his voice.

"That he might ask me why I was the only one to survive the Lions' attack," he said with a trembling voice. "So far no one has asked me that question, and I'm afraid my answer would put our family on the inside of the security fence instead of the outside."

"Gabriel, is there something you haven't told me?" Naomi asked as she heated the pot roast and fixings in the microwave. She buttered two slices of bread and placed them on a napkin in front of him.

"I was frightened when the lions attacked and did the only thing I knew to do," Gabriel said as tears rolled down his face. "I dropped my weapon, knelt and prayed. Moreover, to this day no one has mentioned it."

Walking over to her husband Naomi hugged him. She whispered, "God was watching over you."

"Wh...what?" Gabriel stammered.

"I have something to tell you about Pastor Eagle," Naomi said as she sat next to him and held his hands.

"My great-grandmother married a Tic-ah-nee-skee, but her maiden name is Eagle. Isaac Eagle is my great-grandmother's brother. He's my great-granduncle."

"Oh, God, no!" Gabriel moaned.

**

"Mayor Monroe, tell me the sequence of events for Friday evening," Keller said.

"We open the gates at six p.m. That gives people plenty of time to be seated. Our local high school band will be playing for the night's event. At 7 p.m., the limousine will bring you and District Overseer Patrick McVile to the platform located on the 50-yard line," Monroe pointed to the platform on a map of the stadium. "Once you and the district overseer climb the stairs to the top of the platform, I will greet you and accompany you to your seats."

"No. I want you to meet us as we're getting out of the vehicle and follow us up the stairs," Keller said with a stern voice.

"Yes, sir. Once you are seated, I will go to the podium and introduce you to the people and then take my seat. After you've completed your message you will, or if you desire I can introduce District Overseer Patrick McVile. He plans the sequence of events for the Games," The mayor pointed out.

"At the completion of the Games, I will return to the podium and thank you and the district overseer for your leadership and presence in our community. Then I bid the people a good night until next month," The mayor said. "I'd appreciate any recommendations you may have to ensure a successful event."

"I'll let you know tomorrow. However, tell me, is there tailgating before the Games?" Keller inquired.

"Yes, there is. It is from 5-6:30 p.m.," The mayor replied.

"Good! We'll be attending and let the people get to know us."

"We?" asked startled Monroe.

"Yes. You, me and Patrick. It will be good PR for the Games," Smiled the district commander.

***

Somewhere outside Salina, a secret meeting was in process. Security was tight. Listening posts were set up half a mile out circling the site and roving patrols with dogs inside the perimeter. Four men huddled around a table looking at a map of Mayes County, and a diagram of the football stadium. The leader, John Tic-ah-nee-skee, and three of his closest friends were going over last-minute details for tomorrow evening's rescue plans.

"One more time," John said. "The Games start at 7 p.m."

"At 7:45 security will bring out Pastor Eagle for execution. As the new district commander finishes talking to Pastor Eagle, the stadium lights will go out, and Seb Willyard will set off the bombs underneath the bleachers and speakers platform creating chaos and confusion." Berry Garner said, his second in charge.

"The people in the bleachers are collaborators, and these people shall reap what they have sown for helping the enemy." Berry leaned over the map and pointed to the northeast corner of the stadium, "The rest of Group A will position themselves here to provide covering fire if needed to keep security pinned down. The explosions should keep security busy for at least five maybe 10 minutes."

"When the explosions happen Group B will split up into two groups. The first group will cut holes in the backside of the new security fence and the chain link fence holding the prisoners," Jim Weaver traced his finger around the perimeter of the stadium before continuing. "The security fence has stone columns and wrought iron fence between those columns. We'll need power saws to cut through. My men will use wire cutters on the chain link fence. The second group will rescue Pastor Eagle and escape with the other prisoners. We'll help with loading the prisoners into the vehicles."

"What about the sparks from the power saws won't someone see them?" Tic-ah-nee-ski asked.

"We'll throw a tarp over the area to be cut. It should hide the sparks," Jim said.

"Okay. Continue."

Jack Lowry leaned over the table and pointed to the west side of the stadium and said, "Group C will have the vehicles in place on the west side of the stadium. At the first explosion, we'll drive up to the fence and start loading the people into vehicles. Once loaded the drivers will take them to their designated drop off points. From there the people will be dispersed throughout the county." Jack hesitated and shook his head before continuing, "I'm still not sure if 5 minutes will be enough time to load 200 plus people into all the vehicles."

"We've got that covered. Secondary explosions will go off in the northern part of the parking lot on the east end if needed. That should produce more fear and confusion in the stadium. If we don't need the secondary, my team will retrieve the charges and disappear into the night," Berry informed Jack.

"Okay. No shooting unless necessary." John looked at Jack and said, "Make sure the lights on the vehicles are off and no speeding when leaving the stadium. We don't want to draw attention to the west side of the stadium. Our primary goal is to free the prisoners and get them to safety."

Looking around the table, John continued, "Secondary goal is to embarrass the leaders of the Liberal Nationalist Party by walking in and taking their prisoners without them aware of what's going on. Strongly emphasize that to your people: do not draw attention to what we are doing. There will be other times we can make lots of noise. All right everyone, it's a go for Friday. God be with us."

***

"Gabriel, how are you this morning?" Naomi asked as her husband strapped on his gun belt. He hadn't spoken to her since she shared about being a member of the local resistance group.

"How am I doing? Let's see: I prayed for God to save me from the lions two months ago and no one asked me how I survived; I'm married to the great-grandniece of the man who is an enemy of the state; my wife joined a resistance group fighting against the new government. I'm confused! I'm scared! That's how I'm doing."

"Are you going to turn me into the authorities?" Naomi asked.

"What? Why would I do that? I've been in love with you since the sixth grade. Today can't get any worse. I have to go. We'll talk more tonight."

Naomi kissed Gabriel as he left for work. "Love you. Have a great day," she said with a sigh of relief and headed to her computer and sent out multimedia messages reading: 'Hey, everyone. Don't forget about the Games tonight. See you there.'

Ding-Dong. Ding-Dong.

"Hello, Betsy!" Naomi exclaimed. "Come on in and have some coffee."

"Hey! Has Gabriel gone to work?"

"Yes, all clear."

"Good. The home gatherings are praying for this evening's success."

"And I've sent the messages out. Everything is all set." Naomi said.

***

"Hello, boys," Mary said, as the two men walked in. The petite blonde owner of the Café continued, "Welcome to Eastside Café! Please, sit anywhere you like."

"Thank you. I'm James Keller. My first time in town. You have a homey place, and I like the decor. I take it, from the pictures, you own some racehorses?" Keller said.

"A few. There are times I've wondered if racing horses pay for the café or the café pays for my love of horses. You have any horses?" Mary asked.

"No. However, I appreciate the beauty of good horseflesh."

"Will you be staying long?"

"I'll be leaving tomorrow. Just here for the Games this evening."

"Well, enjoy your stay. Megan will be your waitress."

James Keller pointed to the back table on the right to his companion and proceeded down the aisle. Taking a seat with his back to the wall Keller surveyed the room, customers, and the location of all the exits.

"Hey, handsome! Your usual drink, Gabriel?" Megan, a beautiful dark-haired young lady of Cherokee descent, asked: "And you sir?"

"Coffee black and small ice water," Keller answered as he picked up the menu.

"I'll be right back with your drinks."

"What's good?" Keller asked.

"Everything. I usually have three eggs over-easy, hash browns, crisp bacon, and b & g."

"B & g?"

"Biscuits and gravy, sir."

"Ah. A hearty breakfast. Sounds delicious."

"It's been a traditional breakfast with the Walker family since Granddad Charles Pinkney Walker's time. He served with the Mounted Texas Rangers during the War Between the States. Granddad died in October 1862 and is buried down by Buffalo Gap, Texas. He loved his breakfast. Said it was brain food to get the morning started and the menfolk have kept that tradition going ever since."

"Tradition is important in family life."

"Gabriel, your usual with b & g?" asked Megan.

"Yes, please."

"And you, sir?"

"I think I'll start a new breakfast tradition this morning. I'll have the same," Keller said.

***

The tailgating was well underway when Mayor Monroe, Patrick McVile, James Keller, and security arrived. District Commander James Keller led the group up and down the rows of vehicles stopping every fifth truck to talk with the people and taste the food.

"Howdy, folks. I'm District Commander James Keller. How are you all doing?"

"Doing fine! I'm Leo Nutter, and this is my wife, Gail. We've been looking forward to this event some two months. Hope all goes well tonight."

"I'm positive we won't have a repeat of the last game," Keller noticed McVile's uncomfortableness at the mention of the previous game. "You folks have a good time."

"Thank you kindly."

The mayor came in close and said Keller, "It's 6:30, and we have time for one more stop, sir."

"You can head on over to the platform and get ready. I'll be there shortly."

"Yes, sir," the mayor said as he sprinted as fast as his short legs allowed from the parking lot to the stadium.

"Good evening, folks. I'm James Keller. Are you all enjoying yourselves?"

"Yes, we're having lots of fun. I'm Seb Willyard," Seb said as he grabbed his cane to stand up. "And these are some of my classmates: Patti Agnew, Margaret Edwards, Debra Smarr, and Sheila Irwin."

"Ladies," Keller said as he shook each of their hands. "You don't look old enough to be celebrating your 50th reunion."

"Keep talking like that young man, and you can spend the rest of the evening with us," Margaret piped up. Everyone laughed.

"Not only are we celebrating our 50th High School Reunion, but tomorrow night's football game will be the 100th anniversary of P. Creek's first football game in 1918. So, we'd be honored if you joined us in a toast for this occasion."

Seb reached inside a cooler and pulled out a bottle of Jack Daniels while Patti handed plastic cups to Keller and McVile. Sheila took the bottle from Seb and poured a little in each cup.

"May I make a toast?" Keller asked.

"Please," Seb responded.

Raising his cup to the group Keller said, "Too your health, your reunion, and may you live long and prosperous. Cheers!"

"Now folks I must leave to attend the Games. Enjoy tonight's event," Keller said, leading the way to the waiting limousine.

"He has no clue how much we're going to enjoy tonight," Debra laughed.

"Okay, as soon as the mayor starts his speech, spread out and set the charges. Remember where you put them in case we don't have to set them off. Now let's enjoy our burgers and another drink."

"Here, here," the ladies hooted as they raised their cups high.

***

The stadium filled up fast. The aroma of the steaks and burgers greeted the people as they entered the stadium.

The excitement had been building for this second event of The Games. The local high school band provided music for the event. Vendors made a killing selling popcorn, roasted nuts and drinks to the crowd. Now the climax of the anticipated game was at hand.

A black limousine appeared from the east entrance of the stadium and continued down the sideline to the fifty-yard line where it stopped in front of a platform. The band played "We Will Rock You." The crowd cheered. The driver jumped out and opened the back-passenger door, and a middle-aged, tall man outfitted in a brown shirt with matching trousers, a black tie, and black combat boots exited the vehicle. A tall similarly dressed man followed. Both waved to the crowd as the town mayor greeted them. They shook hands then climbed the stairs to the top of the platform and took their seats.

Mayor Henry H. Monroe moved to the podium once the band had finished and addressed the people. "Ladies and gentlemen. We are here this evening to celebrate the victory over our enemies. These Enemies of the State have eroded our way of life. They have led many astray with their false beliefs and denied all Americans their right to Life, Liberty, and Pursuit of Happiness. However, all that changed, when true American Patriots stood up and said 'No more!' So they took back control of all the American people. Tonight, two of these American Patriots are with us. I introduce to you our District Commander James Keller and Patrick McVile, District Overseer of the Games."

The crowd gave a standing ovation to the honored guests. Once again, the two men waved to the people, then the district commander approached the podium.

"Thank you all for the warm reception. We've come a long way in our battle against our enemies. However, people like you, here tonight, made the fighting much easier. We have been able to disband all political parties and have outlawed all church denominations. We have a new party. There is but one party, and that is the Liberal Nationalist Party. We worship no other god but the Liberal Nationalist Party." The crowd erupted with shouts of joy while the band struck up another tune.

"Thank you again. The Enemies of the State are running, but we will never stop hunting them down. Tonight, we will give some of them an opportunity to renounce their affiliation with these outlaw parties," Keller said, pausing for effect. "Because we are a benevolent party, we will also give Christians a chance to renounce their faith in their false god. Those that renounce their affiliation and faith will be sent to re-education camps and later returned home as obedient and productive citizens of the Liberal

Nationalist Party. Those prisoners who do not renounce we will execute. Here. Tonight." The crowd went wild.

The district commander pointed to the ten-foot high-security fence with razor wire on top surrounding the playing field. Inside stood 500 men, women and children. The prisoners were weeping and wailing. Parents were holding up their children, begging for mercy. Others were falling prostrate on the ground, no longer having the strength to stand on their own.

These people had been rounded up and held in concentration camps scattered throughout Oklahoma for the past seven months. During that time they had not showered nor changed clothing. The aroma of their collective filth and body odor drifted over the stadium causing the witnesses to tonight's game to wave their hands in front of their noses to ward off the stink.

"These are the first of thousands in Oklahoma, who will play in these monthly events. I now introduce to you Mr. Patrick McVile, District Overseer of Northeastern Oklahoma."

Mr. McVile took his place at the podium. "Thank you, District Commander. Let the games begin."

The band played "We Will Rock You" one more time.

The stadium rocked as if the people were watching the Super Bowl playoff.

Holding up his hand to silence the crowd, the District Overseer turned to the people on the playing field. Before speaking, he motioned to a group of security personnel standing near the goal post at the east end of the stadium. Two security guards standing about fifteen feet apart held up flags. The rest formed two columns behind the flag bearers, leaving a pathway to a gate. On the other side of the gate were buses that would take some of the people to the re-education camps.

"When you hear your name called, you will step forward before the platform and make your decision to renounce your party affiliation or church denomination or not. If you renounce, you will immediately head to the eastern end of the stadium"— he pointed to the right — "And board the buses which will transport you to the re-education camp. While in the re-education camp you will be indoctrinated in the ways of the Liberal Nationalist Party. Your progress, or lack of, will determine the length of your stay. If you refuse to renounce, you will go to the western end" — then pointed to his left— "and stand inside the smaller caged area."

The District Overseer motioned for the mayor to join him at the podium.

"Mr. Mayor, it will be your duty, as an obedient and faithful citizen of the Liberal Nationalist Party, to call the names listed on this roster." He held up a binder filled with 500 names. "And you will ask them three questions. First, are you or any of your family affiliated with any outlawed political party? Second, are you or any of your family members of any outlawed church denomination? Third, do you renounce your affiliation or faith in the above mentioned? You will write down their responses. Their final response will determine which direction you point them to."

Taking hold of the binder the mayor approached the podium.

"When I call your name," the mayor said, "step forward in front of the podium. Able; Dennis, Linda, and daughter Lucy. Are you or any of your family affiliated with any outlawed political party?"

"Yes!"

"Are you or any of your family members of any

outlawed church denomination?"

"Yes!"

"Do you renounce your affiliation or faith in the above mentioned?"

"No! You and your liberal jackass friends can go to hell!" Dennis said defiantly.

"That's a no. Go to the cage," The mayor responded as he pointed to his left.

"No! No! I don't want to die!" His daughter cried. "I don't want to leave my friends. Please, father. Don't let me die."

Linda hugged her daughter and looked at Dennis with pleading eyes. He stared at them for several moments and said to the mayor, "My wife and daughter renounce their affiliation and faith. I do not renounce." The mayor pointed to the right for the mother and daughter and to the left for the father.

Dennis glanced at his wife and daughter one last time and headed to the cage with shoulders squared and head held high.

"Attwood; Carl and Darlene…"

***

Pastor Eagle greeted each condemned person as he or she entered the cage with a word of encouragement. Some joined the cage crying and some with broken souls. However, most entered the cage defiantly, not accepting the authority of the new government. When the mayor read the last of the names, he left the podium. Eagle asked everyone in the cage to gather around him.

"We're here because we have defied the new government, some for political reasons and some for religious beliefs. I have been praying these last two months for God to give me answers to many questions I have. I received an answer to one of my questions last night. No one in this cage will die tonight. I don't know how or why, but I do know that when it happens, be quiet, be ready, and be quick to respond. Does everyone understand?"

The prisoners nodded.

"Good. Let's pray," Eagle said as he knelt on the ground.

***

"Everyone in place?" Tic-ah-nee-ski asked.

"Group A in place," Berry Garner said.

"Group B ready," Reported Jim Weaver.

"Group C all set," Jack Lowry responded.

"Maintain radio silence until you hear from me."

***

District Commander James Keller stepped up to the podium and motioned to Security Chief Walker to bring Pastor Eagle out from the cage and onto the field.

Walker led a ten-man security team to the cage where Pastor Eagle knelt in prayer. However, they were stopped dead in their tracks. Something prevented them from advancing. A bright light began emanating around the old man and the prisoners, causing everyone in the stadium to shield their eyes.

The light shone so brightly even the district commander had to shield his eyes.

Not again, thought Walker *a repeat of last time security tried to get Pastor Eagle. What do I do now?*

Standing up, Eagle looked at Walker and nodded. Facing the prisoners, he said, "Remember, be quiet, be ready, and be quick to respond."

The light faded as Pastor Eagle left the cage and walked to the middle of the football field with Walker and the security team trailing. District Commander Keller motioned for the security team to return to their post leaving Eagle alone on the ground.

"Mr. Eagle. You have been found guilty of the death of District Commander Terri McVile by the Liberal Nationalist Party. You are sentenced to death by having your head, arms and legs ripped from your body. See those five four-wheelers at the east end of the stadium? In a minute they will surround you, and someone will tie a rope to each of your limbs and attach the ropes to the four-wheelers. When District Overseer McVile gives the order, the four-wheelers will slowly pull you apart until you are dead. Do you have any last words?" Keller asked.

"I am praying for your soul, Herr Keller."

"I told you no pray..." Suddenly the stadium lights shut off, followed by a series of explosions. *Boom! Boom! Boom! Boom! Boom! Boom! Boom!* The center portions of the north and south stadiums collapsed inward trapping people under tons of debris. People screamed for help. Security ran to help the people.

In the chaos, Pastor Eagle was left unguarded.

***

"All groups get ready." Tic-ah-nee-skee looked at Seb and said, "It's a go. Blow it!" *Boom! Boom! Boom! Boom! Boom! Boom! Boom!*

Berry Garner's group took up position providing covering fire for the rescuers were discovered. Seb and his crew were ready to blow the east side parking lot if things got out of hand. "Group A in place," Berry responded.

The platform holding the mayor and guest speakers

shuttered and came crashing down into the rubble of the stadium, spilling them on top of injured people.

Jim Weaver gave the command for his group to cut through the wrought iron fence with metal saws. Once through, the group split into two teams. Team One cut the chain link fence and started pulling the prisoners out. Team Two, consisting of four men, cut out another section of wall and sprinted to Pastor Eagle, grabbing him they carried him to a waiting car. "Package has left," Jim informed Tic-ah-nee-ski.

Jack Lowry had his people open the car doors as the prisoners came out and shoved them inside. They tapped on the door window signaling for the driver to take off. Jack looked at the time: *5 seconds to load five to eight people per vehicle; a total of 35 cars, trucks and vans for 250 people should be done in under five minutes. Good.* His men guided the prisoners farther down to the waiting vehicles and shoved them inside.

Once the rescued prisoners were gone Jack radioed in "Group C gone."

Jim called in "Group B leaving." Leaning out the car window he asked, "Jack, you coming or you gonna' walk?"

Jack jumped in the front seat and said, "Hey, this old man doesn't walk when he can ride. Now I'm ready for a cold beer."

"Okay, guys let's go," Berry said as he radioed Tic-ah-nee-ski, "Group A leaving."

"Roger! Good work," Tic-ah-nee-ski responded. "Seb, it's time to go. Have your girls collect the unused packages and head home."

Giving thumbs up, Seb radioed his team, "Collect the packages and head home."

***

Security Chief Walker was thrown to the ground as the stadium exploded around him. Shaking his head, he wondered what had happened as he picked himself up. *What happened to the lights? Must get the lights on.*

"Webber, where are you?"

"Here, chief."

"Grab another guard and get the lights back on."

"Aye, chief."

"Davis?"

"I'm right here chief."

"Call 911. Tell them there's a lot of dead and injured."

"Roger, chief."

Picking up his radio, Walker contacted the other security members "Listen up! Turn on your flashlights and start helping the injured. If they can walk, send them to the field. If they're able, have them help with the injured. Help is on the way."

"Harold! Thompson! Come with me."

They carefully made their way to the platform and searched through the debris looking for Keller, McVile and the mayor. Looking at the platform, Walker wondered how anyone could have survived.

"I found the mayor," Harold hollered. "He's dead."

"Over here," Thompson yelled. "McVile is dead, too."

Walker heard a moan to his left. "Bring your lights over here." Shining their lights around, they found the district commander partially covered by the floor of the platform. "You two lift that floor, and I'll pull the commander out. Ready! Lift!" Walker pulled Keller out. Keller screamed and passed out.

"Shine your lights on him while I check him out," Walker ran his hands over the commander and found both his legs broken. "The paramedics will have to take care of the broken legs. Thompson, you stay here and guard the commander and if the commander wakes, up call me on the radio. Harold, come with me."

"Help will be arriving soon. You latch on to the first ambulance and get the medical people over to the commander. If they refuse, tell them that a high-ranking Liberal Nationalist Party is injured and if he dies, they will be participants in the next Game. Got it?"

"Got it, chief," Harold smiled.

The lights came on, and Walker surveyed the carnage all around him. Body parts were lying all over the field and on the stadium. *This disaster is much worse than two months ago when the tigers attacked his men instead of Pastor Eagle* he thought.

Eagle! I forgot all about him when the explosions went off. He looked to the west and saw the empty cage. The prisoners were gone. Pastor Eagle was missing. Running to the cage, he noticed the openings in both fences. Walker collapsed against the chain link fence and shook his head in disbelief.

"Oh. God! I was wrong. My day just got worse. Now we're in real trouble with the Liberal Nationalist Party," Walker said as he forced himself to turn his attention back to the rescue of the injured.

2. THE ACCOUNTANT
By PAUL G BUCKNER

My name is Danny Costello. I grew up on Long Island. How I got *here*, well… that's a long story, but that's where I need to start. From the beginning. You see, I'm a nice guy. Always ready to lend a hand. I like being helpful. I'm also an average fella at five-foot-nine and a buck forty on the hoof, give or take some change. Though I could lose a few pounds, I'm still an average Joe. Black hair, brown eyes - nothing extraordinary about me. Not really, anyways. I blend into the crowd. I work hard, keep my head down and mind my own business. That's about it. I've always been honest, always will be, that's why my story is so hard to believe. Trust me, I get that, but it's all true.

I never thought I would end up in the Midwest, but that's where I ended up, and in all my forty-two years this is the last place I ever expected to be. Podunk, Oklahoma. The middle of the country. Halfway to the west coast.

Halfway to the east coast. I moved here just a year ago so I don't know many people. Circumstances brought me here, work. I'm an accountant by trade and I handle several accounts for my firm. Handled, I should say. I'm good at my job. *Was*, good at my job. I'm a numbers kind of guy. I should start at the very beginning.

It all started late one afternoon. I was going over one of my many rotating accounts, the JNP...er that's short for Jinxx-Norman Petroleum. I found a mistake or what I thought was a mistake so being the honest, *and don't forget helpful kind of guy I am*, I took it to my boss.

"Bring me the file," the suit sitting across from me with the blank look on his face said as he turned to the only window in the room. When he turned back to me, he folded his arms across his chest and nodded for me to continue.

Mr. Frailey, er...my boss, wasn't one to mince words and that afternoon was no exception. He was already in a foul mood. So, I brought him the file. I was feeling pretty good about myself that I had found a mistake that no one else had seen before. When I handed it to him he looked it over for all of three seconds before tossing it down on his desk seemingly uninterested, like what I had found wasn't important or he thought I was wrong. That's when it all went downhill.

...

"I'll take care of this one, Costello. I want you to get to

work on the Darwin account. Close the door on your way out."

I've learned in the short time being with the company when to keep my mouth shut which was whenever Mr. Frailey was in a bad mood, which was most of the time. I left his office and returned to my desk. I pulled up the Darwin account and began working on it. For all of five minutes. Then I guess you could say curiosity got the better of me. I opened the JNP file and started digging deeper. An hour later my heart beat so hard that it felt like my chest was going to explode. In retrospect I should've left it alone, but I couldn't help myself. I knew I was right about those books, and I know that what I saw was only the tip of the iceberg. I mean, cash was being siphoned off into offshore accounts over several years by the pennies, but it added up to millions! Sure, it was small potatoes here and small potatoes there, but it wasn't small errors! Nothing *small* about it; it was enormous. Huge. Colossal.

You should understand, the accounting firm I work for has hundreds of clients and dozens of accountants. We all work on all the accounts as they need processing. It's great for efficiency. You know if someone is out a day or two for sick leave or vacation, another accountant can go in and work on the account, no surprises, no big deal. We handle hundreds of accounts for clients all over the world, but there's a deep, dark secret that I stumbled on to that day and I figured out why my company did that.

I was nervous as a long-tailed cat in a room full of rocking-chairs and needed to calm down, so I left my desk and went to get some air, smoke a cigarette and take it all in. My company had been cooking the books for Jinxx-Norman for years. Sure, a penny or two here and a penny or two there may go unnoticed or seem insignificant, but I like those pennies to match up. Someone from my firm with or without the knowledge of JNP was trickling millions to off-shore shell companies.

When the realization hit me, I nearly lost my breakfast. What I had stumbled onto was crazy illegal. I finished my cigarette and headed back to my desk. When I sat down and woke my computer back up, I was timed out of the account. You know what I mean?

"Yeah, my computer does that when I'm away for more than a few minutes too, very annoying. Continue your story," the suit said as he made a few notes.

When I went to log back in, a big red text box flashed up, *ACCESS DENIED*. I looked around the office. No one seemed to notice me. Or, so I thought. I just happened to turn the direction of Mr. Frailey's office. He was at his window looking at me. When he saw me look back, he closed the blinds.

I looked at the clock and noticed I had missed lunch altogether. I tried logging in to the Darwin file and had no issues so I ducked my head and worked on that file for the rest of the afternoon. When I clocked out, my head was still spinning even worse.

As I drove home, I wondered if I had made a mistake by going to my boss. I told myself that I was just being paranoid. That's all it was, just worried over nothing. I passed by several small mom and pops and began to relax a little, my nerves calming down. When I saw a sign for an electronics store I remembered that I needed batteries for my TV remote. I pulled in. There were only a few vehicles in the parking lot so I figured it would be a quick in and out. I parked near a black Lexus in the back. I remember when I got out I had a weird feeling, you know? Like someone was watching me or something. A bit paranoid, I'm sure, but I wasn't wrong as it turns out. 'Course I didn't know for certain at the time. Anyways, I walked to the front door and just as I put my hand on the handle to open it, a lady comes pushing past me like she didn't even see me. If she did, she didn't seem to care that she almost bowled me over. I said, *excuse me,* but she wasn't paying any attention to me, the lady had her own problems I'm sure. Sorry, I digress a little, but it's the little things that stick with ya, you know? Anyways, I got my batteries and I split. Couldn't shake that feeling I was being watched though. Weird. A few minutes later I pulled into my own driveway, parked and walked inside my rented two-bedroom craftsman on rubber legs.

My house was nothing to write home about as the saying goes. Just in an old, but quiet neighborhood. I don't have much in the way of furniture, don't need much. I sat down on the new but cheap sofa that I found at a consignment store in town and mulled over the day's events. It had to be reported. If I didn't report it and it all came out, I could lose my license as an accountant. I wouldn't be able to work in this state or back home. I wouldn't be able to work in any state for that matter!

My stomach rumbled and suddenly I realized I hadn't eaten anything all day. I didn't have anything in the fridge and I didn't feel like cooking anyway. So, I thought I'd run downtown to a fast food place and grab a burger. I grabbed my jacket and headed out the door. My thought was as I jumped in my car that I would hit the nearest drive-thru where I could take it home and watch TV and eat dinner. I drove around a bit before I finally decided on that little burger joint on the highway. It was the least crowded. A cute, button-nosed redhead handed me my order, but I wasn't in the mood for flirting. I thanked her and drove off. Before I could pull out onto the highway, I had to wait on an approaching vehicle. It was a pickup truck, a dually, as they refer to them out here because of two wheels on each side of the rear end. I pulled out behind him and followed him for a ways when I saw one of his inside tires suddenly go flat. I flashed my headlights at him and waved out the window to pull over several times before he finally noticed me. When he did, I saw he wasn't alone. There was a woman with him. I pulled over behind them on the weed covered shoulder. When they got out to see what the problem was, I let him know that he had a flat.

"Damn, of all the places," he said. "Names Jim and this is my girlfriend Kate."

"I'm Danny. Yeah, sure sounds like you and I have the same kind of luck – all bad," I laughed. "Can I give you a hand? Maybe call a wrecker or something," I suggested, holding my cell phone up to him.

"Nah," he said, looking around, "I can change a flat myself, but I'd rather not do it right here by the highway."

I noticed the parking lot at one of the many refineries was empty and the gate was open. He could pull in there and have plenty of room to work on it and not worry about traffic.

"Would that empty lot work?" I suggested, pointing with my cell again.

"Yeah, perfectly."

I followed them the few hundred yards or so.

He drove slowly on the flat so as not to ruin his rim and pulled in and parked near what appeared to be an office door, though no lights were on inside. I helped him get his jack out.

"Maybe this isn't such a good idea, don't want anyone thinking we're trying to steal anything," Jim said.

I looked around then pointed out the security camera above us.

"As long as we're in coverage of that, they'll know that we're just fixing a flat."

"Yeah, probably so. Might as well get to it. What can they do anyway but ask us to leave," he said?

So, there I was, being a good Samaritan. It was getting late in the evening, but in the dusk, you could still see pretty good. And like I said, the story of my life is all about luck, unfortunately for me it's typically bad! I am the living, breathing proverb, if it weren't for bad luck, I'd have no luck at all.

I was thinking about my luck when two black SUV's suddenly came screeching into the parking lot, and several guys in suits jumped out with guns drawn charging towards us. They shouted for us to get on the ground. This was like a scene out of a bad crime show on TV or something.

"We're just changing a flat," I tried explaining, but they weren't having it. One of the men, a bruiser of a jackass the size of the Rock with a scar on his chin, slammed me to the ground and stuck his gun to the back of my head. I could feel his hot breath on my ear as he leaned down, putting all his weight into the middle of my spine.

"Say another word, and I end you right here for resisting."

I didn't say another word, of course, but I damn near pissed myself. The men held us face down on the concrete at gunpoint until another car pulled in. I never saw the guy's face when he got out, but I could see the door of a black Town-Car open and a man's legs. I could also hear his footsteps as he walked toward us. At first, I thought they were just security, it's their job, and soon they'll know that it was merely a misunderstanding, especially on my part being the Good Samaritan that I am. I was wrong. When the new guy arrived, he had a short conversation with one of his men. I heard them talking but couldn't make anything out. The next thing I know our hands are zip-tied behind our backs, we're stood on our feet and shoved toward the SUV's.

"Where are you taking us? I haven't done anything

wrong!" I said.

That's when the guy that put me on the ground the first time punched me square in the stomach, doubling me over in pain. I panted for breath as he shoved me into the back seat. *They have no right to be doing this, it's kidnapping, and that's a federal offense*, I kept thinking.

Two more men jumped into the front seat as my new friend slid in the back with me so that he could jam his gun into my rib cage. He wasn't gentle with that either. He clasped a hand across my face and glared at me.

"I told you to shut up. That's exactly what I mean," he said, shoving my head up against the window.

His hand was like a vice grip, I thought he was going to break my jaw. He had on black leather gloves. I knew that from the smell. I thought it odd, but I complied and stopped struggling, though my eyes never looked away. His voice was low and guttural. Cliché as hell. The kind you hear bad actors use in movies, but in this case I knew he meant it. I glared at him. That only made him push his gun into my ribcage harder and tighten his grip even more. My look of protest turned to fear and compliance.

"There, there. That's a good boy," he said and patted my cheek when he let go. "You don't want a piece of me. Do you? Nah, not a little guy like you, eh?"

I just looked at him. I wasn't turning away, though I wasn't glowering at him. He reached into his pocket and pulled out a butterfly-knife and waved it in my face. My expression changed from pissed off to worry, fear, even! That's what he was after, and he got it. I was probably shaking so hard my teeth were chattering to be honest. The guy was a masochist. He was enjoying it.

He pushed me forward and cut the zip tie, swished that butterfly knife around several times like Bruce Lee and put it back in his pocket. You know, showing off that he was an expert on using it.

"Here ya go big guy," he said. He turned his pistol around and tried handing it to me. The driver snickered. The other guy riding shotgun up front sat quietly watching this all take place, never said a word.

I was confused by the move. Was he trying to test me, see what I would do? If he were a security guard or a cop he wouldn't take the chance. Would he?

"Go on, I said. Take it!" he growled. He grabbed my hand and shoved the gun into it. "There, how's that feel big man?" he asked.

The weight of the gun was more than I expected. I never held one before. Somehow, I think he knew that.

"Go ahead, what are you waiting for?"

I looked at the two guys in the front seat. I could see the driver watching us in the rearview mirror. His eyes glinted coldly.

"He's not got it in 'im, Joe."

I heard the driver say in a croaky voice. My heart drummed hard against my chest, trying to break out it seemed. I held the gun up with trembling hands. I couldn't help but think about the Andy Griffith television shows. You know the ones, where Barney's hands were always shaking like a maple leaf in a heavy wind. It's funny what your mind does in high-stress situations. I could barely hold on to the weapon with one hand. I clasped it between both, but again was too shaky. I let go of it, and he snatched it back and turned it back on me.

"Yeah, didn't think so," he said smugly. "Now, sit back and relax but keep your damn mouth shut."

It was dark by then as we drove out of town. At first, I thought they were taking us to a corporate office. I tried looking out the window to see where we were going, but I really couldn't tell. Being new to the area, once they turned off the highway, I was lost. The tinting on the windows kept me from seeing much anyway. We traveled down old dirt roads and pot-holed black-tops off and on. There was no way I could count all the twists and turns they made. We even crossed over a bridge at one point. I knew what it was from the clickety-clack of the old wood. I was beginning to understand. When we passed over that bridge and turned onto a bumpy dirt road, I knew I was going to have to do something because if I didn't, I was going to die. These men weren't driving us out here for the scenery. They aimed to kill us! Why? I don't know, but that's the only reason for taking someone out into the country like this, secluded, far away from town, far away from the authorities. It suddenly dawned on me - this had to be about me. It had to be about the Jinxx-Norman file. My boss tipped someone off. It wasn't about us being in the wrong place at the wrong time; it wasn't about fixing a flat tire. Poor Jim and Kate got caught up with a snitch, a whistle-blower!

Eventually the driver pulled up and stopped in a wooded area, and I was shoved out. When I stumbled out, I saw that Jim and Kate were standing outside still tied up. Jim looked like they had roughed him up, but he was still defiant. Much braver than me, I promise. The one they called Joe shoved me over to stand with them. That's when I noticed the parking permit of the SUV, Jinxx-Norman Petroleum.

"Get over there," he growled.

I stumbled on rubber legs and bumped into Kate. She stumbled too but Jim was there and did his best to catch her, but with his hands zip-tied behind him there wasn't much he could do. She fell to her knees and then one of the goons jerked her back up.

"Why don't you bastards drop the gun and see what happens!" Jim said.

One of the men walked over and slugged him over the head with the butt of his gun. A flash of blood spurted from a nasty gash he opened on Jim's forehead. Kate screamed. Jim staggered and struggled to stay on his feet. Kate was crying, begging and pleading for them to stop.

I knew I couldn't wait any longer. I had to make a break for it just as soon as I found an opening. I had to get away and get help. These people meant to kill us.

"Shut her up, or I'll do it for ya!" one of the men demanded. He was a mean looking sort. Had a small nose, slits for eyes and pinched cheeks that were redder than the color of the tan that the rest of his face had. His brow was thick and heavy. I dunno, kinda reminded me of what Cro-

Magnon man would've looked like. But all six of the bastards had guns in their hands.

"Please, whatever it is that you want from us just take it and let us go," Jim said, as he spat blood out.

"Let you go? Nah, we can't do that. You were caught red-handed trespassing on private property. Haven't you ever heard of the *Stand My Ground* law?" the man sneered. He punched Jim in the gut so hard that it knocked him to his knees.

Kate was a sobbing mess at that point. I knew if there were any breaks, she was going to be worthless. Too petrified to move. No, I couldn't take the chance of worrying about them. It was each man on their own.

"That was very noble and chivalrous of you," suit said sarcastically, interrupting my story.

"Yeah, well, you see how far that got me."

The man moved toward Jim again and grabbed him by the hair and hoisted him up straight.

"Stand up and act like a man," he sneered.

Jim glared back defiantly. He had plenty of fight in him, and I'm sure if they didn't have guns and he wasn't tied up, he coulda done some serious damage.

"Please," Kate begged them. "Leave us alone."

In an instant, the guy let go of Jim and slapped her across the face with his gun hand. Her shriek was loud and echoed through the woods. Jim must've broken the zip tie somehow because he jumped up and punched the guy square in the nose. I saw the blood splatter.

"You son of a bitch, I'll kill you," Jim shouted.

It drew the attention of all the goons and left me unguarded. That was my chance to make a break for it. I shoved one of the men as hard as I could into the others and bolted for the woods. I ran between the SUV's putting the vehicles between them and me. It was dark as hell in the middle of the woods. The headlights of the SUV's were still on, shining straight ahead, but they did me no good the further away I ran. I heard several gunshots though not in my direction. Kate wasn't screaming anymore.

A man shouted orders behind me.

"Find him! Now!" I heard him say. I ran as fast as I could. I heard heavy footsteps coming behind me and then more gunshots. I felt a bullet zing past me and then another exploded into a tree near me. I zig-zagged through the trees, branches slapped at my face and ripped through my flesh. I knew I was getting cut up and banged to hell, but I was still alive. I didn't care; I was running for my life. Adrenaline pushed me. I was gaining some distance on the bastards, but how much I didn't know. I just kept running. I'm entirely out of shape so I was breathing hard, but knew better than to stop. I didn't want to slow down, but my body wasn't paying attention to my head. Honestly, my running wasn't probably more than a fast walk to most people at that point.

The sky was cloudy that evening so what little moon there was, was obscured. Earlier that day it had threatened to rain and I hoped that it would hold off. Even though it was late Fall, it wasn't unusually cold yet, but a cold November rain could sure change that. It had rained the previous night and the ground was still wet. I thought it could work for me and against me at the same time. On the one hand, the dead leaves on the ground were soft, damp and quiet to step on. On the other, my tracks would be visible to my pursuers if they had flashlights. I remember thinking that surely, they didn't. Why would they?

I must have stumbled and fallen a dozen times if once, but I wasn't stopping. I couldn't. My lungs burned, screamed for oxygen. Thirty years of smoking tends to do that to a fella. Well, that, and never working out a day in my life might have something to do with it. All I could hope for was to evade getting shot by the aid of darkness and lady luck. I didn't know how long I had been in the woods, but at that point I didn't care. When I thought that I had run as far as I could and had enough distance between them, I stopped to rest and try to get my bearings. I collapsed to the ground, gasping for air trying to calm my nerves. I lay as quiet and motionless as possible listening for any sign that they were near, but my heart beat so hard and fast, that was the only thing I could hear. I couldn't see a thing except when the clouds parted and the moonlight shined through. Even then, all I could make out was the vague outline of trees.

I was sweating and the night chill was beginning to set in. I was tired and sore as hell. I was surprised my heart hadn't given way yet and simply exploded as it beat like a steaming locomotive inside my ripped up and soaked shirt. I couldn't tell if the wetness was sweat or blood, but I had a feeling it was both, my adrenaline just wouldn't let me feel the pain yet. But I knew the wet stickiness on my face was blood. Running blind through the woods is not a pleasant experience. Every little branch seems to reach out in the darkness to rip at your flesh. Briars, tree limbs and who knows what else.

As I sat there in the middle of the woods jumping at every little sound, I thought to myself, *what could I do to save my own life. What was I capable of?* I honestly had no idea. They took our cell phones so I had no way to call the police for help. I had no idea where they had driven us so even if I had my cell, I wouldn't know where to direct them. This deep in the boonies, I doubt there was any cell service anyway. No, I had to find the road. I had to get to the police. That was my only chance. Expose them and live. Maybe.

I had to get moving. I dragged myself up using the tree to lean against and then listened for any sounds of pursuit. As soon as the clouds parted allowing a sliver of moonlight through, I saw a bit more of the trees around me. I ran. As far as I knew, I could be straying deeper and deeper into those woods. I stumbled along and tried to reason it out the best I could under the given circumstances. I had a few options. The first one, I could hunker down until morning when I had some daylight to work with. In which case, it may also give those security guys time to call in reinforcements and track me down. That didn't sound fun.

Option two, I could keep going in hopes that I could find the road and find my way out of there. Of course, that meant taking a chance that I didn't stumble right back into them by walking in circles. I got my answer when I felt the chill of a cold wind blow across my face. Colder than earlier. A moment later, it started raining. Softly, but enough to get through what little canopy the bare limbs of Fall had on the trees. I had to keep moving or die from hypothermia. *Just great*, I thought. *Could it get any worse?*

I stumbled along still unable to see clearly, still tripping, falling and getting cut up by branches that I couldn't see. Luckily, I hadn't broken anything yet or fell off a cliff. I stopped to rest a moment and leaned against a tree. I thought I heard something but wasn't sure what it was. I took off again, and the noise seemed to get louder. It sounded like rain, but the rain was not much more than a sprinkle. I could plainly hear the pitter-patter of the rain. No, that wasn't rain, it was more like…like churning.

Suddenly, my feet shot out from under my legs, and I slid headfirst down an embankment splashing into the river. The rain was cold, but the flowing river was colder, much more frigid. The bank was sloped and muddy. I never saw it in the dark, but I realized what it was way too late. If the constant pounding of a stress-filled heart wasn't going to do me in, the dramatic traumatization of a polar-plunge would surely do the trick. I came up gasping for breath. Using every ounce of strength I could muster, I scrambled out using anything I could get my hands on - rocks, limbs, mud. I clawed my way to the top of the embankment and curled up in the fetal position hugging those rain-soaked leaves and shivered. I'm sure if you could've seen me, I would've been a pleasant shade of blue.

I guess I must've fallen asleep at some point. It was still dark when I woke up by the river, and I was still cold. I had hoped that it had all been a bad dream, but that wasn't the case. My muscles ached, and my body was so stiff that it hurt to move, but I knew I had to. I had to get up and keep moving. I raised up on my hip and elbow, then felt around for anything to grab. A nearby tree branch was all I found. It did the trick. I was back on my feet, but what now? Though it wasn't raining anymore, I had the little problem in front of me of the river. I damn sure didn't want to fall into that again. I'd never survive a second dunking. I could just make out the silhouettes of the trees and the banks, so I backed away from the river and decided to try and follow it the best I could. Maybe I could find the bridge, cross over and then make my way to the highway.

Making sure the coast was clear as the saying goes, I started off at the fastest pace my stiff legs would carry me. At that point, I didn't care about all the limbs slapping at my face or the rocks and branches I tripped over. My goal was to parallel the river until I found a road. I plodded along like that for a while. Soon, I stumbled out on to a muddy but visible roadway. I turned and saw the bridge and kept going. I knew I was moving at a snail's pace, but at least I was moving, and that's all I could ask for. My body was beaten to hell and damn near frozen solid. I couldn't feel my legs anymore. Hell, I couldn't feel anything, but I knew if I stopped, I might never get going again. I got across the bridge and kept going.

When I came to the highway, I recalled that the last turn the driver took before crossing the bridge was a left. I turned right and prayed a vehicle would come by. A big semi-truck. Anything else and I would have to scurry off the road and hide; it could be the bastards looking to kill me. I reasoned that if it were a big semi, I should be safe and possibly catch a ride to the police station. That was my thinking anyway.

I never heard or saw the police cruiser pull up behind me until he turned on the red and blue lights and hit the *woop-woop* of the siren a few times to get my attention. It scared me. When I tried to turn around to look, I stumbled and fell. I was staring into the headlights. The cascading red and blue whirling – spinning - flashing, well, that's the last thing I remember.

"Uh huh, is that it?" the detective sitting across from me asked.

"Yeah, what more do you need to make an arrest?" I asked.

"Oh, I think that'll do," he said.

There was a knock at the door. The detective stood, walked to it and opened it. Someone in the hallway handed him something and a few whispers later, he closed the door and came back to sit again. Sliding a handgun onto the table inside a plastic bag.

"Does this look familiar?" he asked.

"Sure. It looks like one of the guns these men had. Could've been the gun they used to kill them with. Maybe."

"What do you mean, maybe?"

"Well, after all, there were five others there, and they all had guns," I replied.

"Uh huh, okay."

The door to the interrogation room opened again. This time the detective just sat and waited while another detective hooked up a television perched on top of a pushcart.

"Just hit play, Bob."

Bob hit play and stepped back. A video flashed up on the screen. At first, I didn't understand what I was looking at. Then it hit me. It was the security footage from the refinery; only it was…different.

"Is that your car on the road flashing your headlights and flagging the truck down?"

"Yes, it is, but how did you get that so fast?"

"Let me ask the questions. Now, there you are pointing what appears to be a gun at the couple in the truck and motioning for them to pull up into the parking lot at the refinery."

"No! That's not a gun, that's my cell phone! What the hell are you talking about? Are you nuts?" I shouted, jumping up from the table.

"Sit down Mr. Costello," Detective Arnez growled. "You can't deny that's your car, and that's you right there in that video waving a gun, *this* gun, at the couple that you murdered, which, by the way, has your prints all over it.

Just yours. No other prints. The gun's been fired recently."

I knew then what was happening. The bastards in the woods didn't care if they found me or not. Either way, I was a goner. They had set me up good.

"You're crazy, I didn't kill anyone," I screamed. "I don't even own a gun let alone know how to shoot a gun." It was pointless to argue, but I had to try. I couldn't take my eyes off the video. "It's been altered," I muttered sinking back into the cold aluminum chair. That's my luck. "It's all been changed."

"In what way? Forensics said it hadn't been altered whatsoever."

"Just keep watching, you'll see the guys in black cars pull up and throw us to the ground."

"Uh huh," he said turning back to the TV.

We watched as I stood there talking to Jim and Kate. When it got to the part where I motioned up at the camera, only a few seconds roll by and the video ends.

"And that's where you took out the camera, but by that time, it was too late. So, here's where we're at, Mr. Costello." The detective stood.

"You flagged down Jim Mayfield and his girlfriend, Kaitlin Webber, who happens to work as a clerk in your office. Nothing suspicious there. That is until we found the file on your desk with a post-it note in your handwriting with her name and with your fingerprints on it. It seems you've been a naughty boy, Mr. Costello, embezzling thousands of dollars. It looks like you've been able to siphon off upwards of fifty-grand from this, um…" he looked at his notes again, "This Darwin account and stashing it in a phony company account under your name. We have the bank records to prove it," the detective said, slamming down another file on the table.

I sat unmoving, unflinching, just staring at the detective's mouth, watching his lips move. There was nothing I could say. I couldn't believe what was happening. I felt helpless.

"Once you thought you were going to get caught, you tried to make it look like Ms. Webber did it. You tried setting her up but failed so you figured you had to kill her. Whether it was dumb luck or lousy luck, she happened to be with her boyfriend so you made it look like a murder-suicide thing, but you didn't count on her boyfriend fighting back."

He must've seen the shock on my face when he said that. "Wait a minute," I said. "I killed them?"

"Yeah, that's right. And now that I have your confession…"

"Confession? I didn't confess a damn thing!" I shouted.

"We have it all pieced together, Costello. Fits perfectly. Better than OJ's glove, better than a jigsaw puzzle. Jim fought back and chased you into the woods. Oh, he didn't make it far, he bled out and died only steps away from Kaitlyn. That's a cold-blooded killer instinct you have. It's a real pleasure to get you off the streets. You'll be headed to death row in no time."

I couldn't speak. Completely dumbfounded. How could I have been so stupid?

"Daniel Costello, you're under arrest for the murder of

Jim Mayfield and Kaitlin Webber. You have the right to remain silent, anything you say will be held against you in a court of law."

I heard the other detective that had wheeled in the television snicker. I looked at his face then. It was none other than the bastard that had shoved the gun into my hand in the black SUV. My heart sank. He was a cop!

3. ZIPTIE

By JULIE JONES

"I'm sorry, but it's cancer. We don't know how long for sure, but estimate you have about six months."

These blunt words still ricocheted around my mind as I entered a small electronics store in Nowhere, Oklahoma. I chose to go ahead as planned with the business trip despite my diagnosis, less than five days old. My company would never have sent me if they knew, not only because of my illness but because the devastating news meant I was a scattered, jumbled mess. My misplaced phone charger was small proof, the first I ever lost. As my eyes scanned the store, I found that sorry bastard instead.

He stood with a store clerk next to a display of Bluetooth speakers, as if he had any right to be living and breathing and shopping like a normal human being. I felt my blood pressure ratchet up, the whoosh drowning out all other sound for a moment. Rotten guts writhed in protest.

My body flushed with righteous, angry heat.

"Which of these has the longest battery life?" His baritone voice made my skin crawl.

That was Jim Knight, the son of a bitch that molested my boy. Twelve years since the blackest time of my life, and I worked hard to put those days behind me. But his ugly face was etched into my brain forever. He examined the wall of speakers and did not see me.

"Oh, hell no." I ducked around a nearby corner to get hold of myself.

The fluorescent lights were harsh, and I screwed my eyes shut. The mellow strains of Tom Petty's "Won't Back Down" rang loud and ironic from the store's hidden speakers. My hand found the zipper of my jacket and began the rhythmic, up-and-down *ziiiip*ziiiip* that felt so familiar and soothing.

Everything flooded back and I struggled to control my breathing.

Jeremy was ten when it began. He was shy, but expressed an interest in camping and the outdoors. My husband Jeff and I put him in the Straight Arrow Club to help our son make friends and get him outside. Jim Knight welcomed the boy into his local chapter with enthusiasm. It was two years before Jeremy told us what was happening.

My stomach clawed at me like a rabid dog, remembering.

The Assistant DA, Arthur Chamfer, was a known crony of Jim Knight and a dozen other questionable figures in the area. He brushed aside any serious charges and bribed the police chief to mishandle the investigation. Jim Knight was considered a respected member of our small Texas community. Most important, he greased a lot of palms and had a lot of connections. Nobody was going to take him on.

You lose, his smug face said, that final day in court. Chamfer wore an expression to match. That day, a small part of my heart turned to stone.

By then almost fourteen, Jeremy's defeated gaze was

heartbreaking when we gave him the news.

"Why is this guy getting away with hurting me?"

It was a question we had no answers for. A grueling year of investigations, interrogations, and litigation yielded nothing. Jim Knight would end up receiving two years' probation for negligence and child endangerment, and his position with the Straight Arrows was dissolved. Nothing else.

"Honey, we have to try to move on." Jeff repeated the phrase like a song stuck on repeat. But soon he was let go from work. His boss blamed 'seasonal layoffs' even though the company had never done such a thing before. Jeff was the only layoff.

Later we found out that the company VP was a good friend of none other than Jim Knight.

Before long I heard mutters about my family all over town. People gossiped and spread lies at the grocery store, the local restaurants, even the library. The bank raised the interest rate on our mortgage. The county assessor, Jim Knight's cousin, appraised our home for an outrageous amount, hiking our property tax through the roof. Jeremy withdrew further than ever, and bullying at school became a serious issue.

Within six months of Jim Knight's probation sentencing we made the reluctant decision to move. Every blow to my family turned another sliver of my heart to stone.

All this flooded back to me as I stood trembling in the aisle of a third-rate electronics store, in the middle of flyover country.

"Just breathe. Just...breathe." I repeated the mantra, dragging my jacket zipper up with Just and down with breathe. My focus was inhaling and exhaling, and the soothing rhythm of the zipper, until I felt myself pull away from the sharp edge of panic.

The thin edge of control I had was shaky, and I stood wondering what to do. Part of me wanted to leave, slink out like a whipped dog and lick my reopened wounds in my car. The larger part of me wanted to charge over and defend my son once again. Emotional overload and indecision gripped me like a vise.

My desperate, searching gaze fell on a clear plastic container of zip ties. They were over two feet long and heavy duty, made of thick black plastic and meant to bundle cords and cables, amongst other uses. I love them. They bring order to chaos and hold things together. The clack clack clack of the ratcheting plastic is soothing.

An absurd thought surfaced that zip ties are all I need. My mind flashed to an image of me picking up the pieces of my life and zip tying them back together.

On impulse I plucked a container of ties off the hook and made my way to the front of the store, toward the register and away from Jim Knight.

"Did you find everything okay, ma'am?"

"Actually I need a charger for my cell phone."

The perky clerk took a quick look at my phone and assured me this was no problem, then disappeared for a long thirty seconds. I prayed that Jim Knight would keep looking at speakers and let me escape.

At last she returned with a new charger in hand. I paid cash for my items and headed for the door, almost knocking over an average-looking man with black hair as he tried to come in.

"Excuse me!"

I ignored his sarcasm and made a beeline for my car, intending to get the hell out of there. Instead, I got in and sat for several long minutes, not thinking.

My mind was blank, yet busy. I felt like television static. The knob in my head was changing channels, looking for a clear signal.

I scanned the parking lot, spotting a sleek black Lexus in the back corner. It was parked in the middle of four spaces to keep away from other vehicles. Jim Knight's exact taste and parking style.

On autopilot, I started my car and circled the lot, coming around behind the Lexus and noting the personalized "KNIGHT" on the tag. This guy still thought a lot of himself. I parked several spots away and killed the engine, not at all sure what I was doing, or why. I opened the package of zip ties and took one out with anxious fingers. The soothing ratcheting sound was loud in the car.

Clack, clack, clack.

I was slow closing the loop, but even with two feet of track I soon ran out and reached into the package for a fresh one. Jeremy had loved them, too. When he was little he would get into his father's tool box and zip tie all the tools together.

He never psychologically recovered from his abuse. As the years passed he pulled away from us, becoming sullen and depressed despite our efforts to get him into counseling. He lost several jobs due to drug use, refused rehab, and involved himself in sketchy activities. We were powerless to help.

Jeff could not find a job in our new city, despite being across the state from our hometown. Jim Knight's shadow followed us, blocking every path and closing every door we sought out. Desperation became our new normal.

Looking back, I blame myself for not doing more. More what, I have no clue, but there had to be something. I risked my own mental and physical breakdown from the constant stress. I suffered permanent exhaustion from looking for some way, any way that would help my family. It was not enough. Now I was paying for it with a decaying belly.

I sat in the parking lot, turning the giant zip tie over in my hands, thinking about Jeremy's last days. He came to see us, his first visit in close to two years. He looked good; eyes alert, with clean clothes and carrying a healthy weight. He said he was ready to leave "the life" behind. Jeff and I were over the moon, hopeful for the first time in forever.

Jeremy might have left behind his life of petty crime and drug use, but it did not leave him. A week after arriving on our doorstep, he was killed by his former dealer for substantial debts.

Jeff found his body in our backyard, face down in a pool of blood.

The sound that came from my husband's throat still haunts my dreams. It was the sound an animal makes when it takes a lethal blow that does not kill right away.

Jeremy's journal was found later. I never read it. Jeff did, and would not speak of what he discovered inside. He seemed both soothed and disturbed by it, and it disappeared from the house soon after. Last I knew, it was buried in a stack of papers in my safety deposit box.

Through the window of the electronics store I could see Jim Knight paying for his purchase and preparing to leave. I ducked down behind the steering wheel and watched.

Once outside, he strode to his car and swung into the driver's seat. Oblivious to my presence, he cranked the engine and threw it into drive at almost the same moment. Mind staticy, I started my car and followed him out of the lot and down the street at a discreet distance.

"What the hell is he doing here?" The windshield did not answer. Blondie belted out "One Way Or Another" on the radio.

This coincidence felt too fateful to be random. This little town was in the middle of Oklahoma, a far cry from our hometown in southeast Texas. I was passing through on business, having been to Kansas to attend a tradeshow. I only stopped to replace my lost phone charger.

Jim Knight was not the sort of man to leave where his nest was feathered. Nor was he the sort to skimp on pampering when it came to his comforts. This tiny town so far from his base of operations was not his style at all. So what was he doing here?

I felt the channel knob in my head settle on a clear signal. The overwhelming flood of hatred I felt toward this man welled up, disconnecting my reasoning. I felt like a television spectator of unfolding events: watching, but with no power to control anything.

My detachment was both terrifying and somehow tranquil. I knew it was wrong, but feeling nothing was better than the constant misery of the last few years.

"Let's see where this asshole is going." The steering wheel complied.

He drove through town and kept going west. A few miles past city limits stood a ramshackle motel with peeling paint and a broken Vacancy sign, sprawled like a long, ugly scar on the side of the road. He turned into the gravel parking lot and I followed at a safe distance, careful to be inconspicuous.

Night had fallen, darkness coming early in January. The parking lot crunched under my tires as I turned in and rolled to a stop at the far end of the building, near the last room. I turned off the engine and reached for the zip tie lying on the passenger seat, resuming my nervous fidgeting.

Without the headlights, darkness flooded my car. The motel's exterior lighting was poor. So many bulbs were out that the only real illumination came from the light streaming through the office windows at the other end of the building.

Jim Knight got out of his car and approached one of the motel rooms. Despite the darkness, his key was quick and he was in the room and closing the door as if by magic. Nothing else moved. I twisted the zip tie in my hands.

My numbed state altered into a sort of hypnosis. Time stretched out. The fire in my midsection subsided to coals. I sat, staring through my windshield at the broken motel sign, flashing " O ACAN Y" in garish neon red. It was so captivating that I was startled at the distant sound of a slamming door.

I spotted Jim Knight striding up the sidewalk, wearing only boxer shorts, heading for the ice machine near the front office. I got out of my car, the sound of the closing door breaking my weird reverie. Zip tie forgotten in my hand, I moved toward the motel room.

The curtain in the window by his door twitched aside to reveal the bruised, terrified face of a young boy, perhaps fourteen, peering into the darkness. I stopped in my tracks.

Pure, white hot fury exploded in my system, sending shock waves along my limbs. The fire in my belly was nothing compared to this. My lungs spasmed and stopped, and my vision went red. I always thought that was just an expression. The zip tie looped in my hands, the first few snicks of it snapping along the track. It failed to soothe me.

He was returning with his bucket of ice. I waited for him to get closer.

"Jim Knight." My voice cut through the darkness like a knife. He startled and dropped the bucket. Ice scattered across the dark gravel like diamonds on velvet.

"Dammit! What the hell? Who are you?"

"You know exactly who I am."

He squinted into the darkness, ice crunching under his feet as he stepped closer to get a better look. His eyes widened in surprise.

"Is that you…?"

"Lilith. I am Lilith."

He guffawed. "I don't know any broads named Lilith."

"I didn't say it was my name. I said it's who I am."

"Whatever, lady. You're nuts."

He dismissed me and turned back to his room. The zip tie came up, looped over his head and around his neck. I yanked the tail as hard as I could.

The satisfying choking sounds that came from his throat were like a balm to my soul. Pulling on the tail jerked Jim Knight backward toward me, and I took the opportunity of his imbalance to get a better grip. The zip tie made bright, snapping sounds as it ratcheted tighter.

He fell to the ground, feet kicking in fear. His head was a bright red ball of blood. His hands scrabbled at his neck, desperate to find any slack or weak spot that would afford him a respite. The zip tie dug into his flesh.

I stood over his panicked, struggling form. He rolled his eyes in my direction.

"Jeremy is dead because of you. Jeff didn't have the will to fight his cancer because of you. That boy in your room is traumatized because of you. No telling who else you've used and abused in your worthless life. And now, you die. You are the sorriest sack of shit that ever lived, and I hope you roast in hell forever."

His feet slowed their hopeless kicking. I watched as he went limp. The realization of what I did began to sink in. I thought I should be descending into my own panic, knowing what my actions were.

Instead, I felt light. Light, for the first time in twelve years.

I returned to my car and fished a pack of antibacterial wet wipes from my purse. I returned to Jim Knight's body and wiped down the zip tie, attempting to remove any evidence that would link me to the scene. I scanned the area for witnesses, but nobody was around. Other than Jim Knight's room, the motel appeared empty.

His phone was in his pocket and I took it. Before walking away, I gave his dead body a good kick in the ribs. He could not feel it but it was cathartic to me. He might be dead, but I still hated him.

I approached the motel room door and rapped twice. I could feel the room go still on the other side. I put my face close to the peeling paint.

"Stay in the room. Help is coming."

No response.

I was careful to leave the parking lot as just another vehicle, innocent and inconspicuous. Over the crunch of tires on gravel, Aerosmith belted out "Janie's Got A Gun" on the radio.

A mile down the road I used Jim Knight's phone to Google the seedy motel's phone number. The clerk picked up on the third ring. I disguised my voice.

"Room eleven has an underage victim of sex trafficking inside." The astonished clerk had no time to respond before I hung up and turned off the phone.

I crossed a bridge about five miles down the road, and tossed his phone into the river below. I felt as if I tossed away part of myself with it.

As I drove, I considered the fact that I may have gone insane. The past several years were rough. I was in a lot of pain and under a lot of stress. I took stock of my intestines and found the pain there, but tolerable.

I must have snapped in the store. How else could I explain to myself what I had done? I was frightened by the fact that I was not appalled. In fact, I could not deny a growing sense of grim justice.

"That monster will never touch another child." The

spoken words were a hymn, hanging in the air like golden curlicues. I said it again, and laughed. A tiny kernel of purpose began to grow in the back of my mind.

I tried to ignore it. I should have been alarmed by my mounting excitement at the idea. Instead, I felt motivated for the first time in years. But what was I thinking? The sort of thing I had in mind is just not done. It has no place in polite society.

Who am I kidding, though? Am I supposed to care about the society that molested my boy, bullied him, protected his abuser, ruined my future, and caused my husband to give up on life? I already took the irrevocable step; I took justice into my own hands and executed my son's molester. Jeremy and Jeff are gone. I have terminal cancer, a tiny apartment, and a dead-end job.

I am the definition of 'nothing to lose.'

Driving down a dark two-lane highway in the middle of nowhere, I embraced Lilith as my new name, shedding the old one like a snakeskin.

It took all night to get home. I was on the weary edge of exhaustion when the key found the knob of my apartment door. Too tired to notice my aching belly, I dropped my bags on the dining table and stumbled to the bedroom.

Six hours and a hot shower later, I opened the new charger, plugged in my phone, and sat at my table with a cup of coffee to check in on the world. After killing Jim Knight, I left my dead cell phone uncharged and off. I spent the drive home listening to the whirring of my own mind. It might not have been my best choice.

I soon discovered that word of Jim Knight's demise in a motel parking lot in Oklahoma already trickled down the local grapevine. I was two minutes into my Facebook feed before seeing my first 'RIP Jim Knight' post. It brought back the searing rage and my belly flared up. I could not believe anyone would mourn this asshole. There would be no one to mourn me, and once I was gone, no one to mourn my Jeremy or my Jeff. The irony was cutting.

My patience for social media spent, the next order of business was checking voicemail. There were the usual scam calls, a couple messages from co-workers, and one from my oncologist.

"This is Dr. Douglas. I need to speak to you as soon as possible. Please call my nurse and schedule to see me. We have things to discuss."

I stared at the table top so long that the automated voicemail attendant gave up on me and disconnected.

"So that's it." The finality was inescapable. My mind went staticy again, and I felt the TV channel in my head change again. My tongue tasted bitter.

Jim Knight deserved to die, and I did not regret my role in it. The big question now was, what would I do next?

The package of zip ties poked out of my travel bag, and I plucked one out. I ran the length of black plastic through my hands, letting my fingernail drag along the strip.

"I'm surprised how well that worked."

I was lucky with my attack on Jim Knight. The scenario was perfect, all elements exactly in place. He turned his back on me with zero suspicion, and I happened to have the zip tie ready, slipping it over his head with laser beam precision. It was a one in a million shot and I could not have been more smooth. No way could I do it again.

"I'm definitely crazy." I took up my phone and scrolled through the call log until I reached my oncologist's number and dialed. I gave the nurse my name and she put me on hold.

A different nurse picked up. "Ma'am, Dr. Douglas wants to see you as soon as possible to discuss treatment options. Would you be able to come in tomorrow at 2:30?"

"Tomorrow? Geez I figured it would be a couple of days."

"No ma'am. He would like to see you as soon as possible."

"That can't be good, can it?"

"I really can't say either way. Only that the Doctor wishes to see you."

"Okay then, pencil me in I guess."

"Very good. I will let the Doctor know. Thank you." She hung up.

I called my office next. The receptionist put me through to my manager, who told me to take until Monday to rest up and get my reports together. My voice was hollow as I thanked him and disconnected. I had no intention of doing any reports.

Nowhere to be until tomorrow and I was off the hook for work. Sounds like a treat for most people, but my lonely apartment felt airless and confining. If I did not leave, I was sure the walls would close in and smash me flat.

I got in the car, intending to drive around for a little while and shake off the anxiety. Wrapped in a fog of thought, I did not tune in to my whereabouts until I passed the welcome sign for my old hometown. Then I knew I was headed for Arthur Chamfer's place.

Chamfer was the Assistant D.A. that mishandled the prosecution of Jim Knight, and ensured the monster got a slap on the wrist. Since orchestrating that miscarriage of justice, he since climbed the ladder to D.A. and then circuit court judge. His residence was well known to the community, being an imposing mansion perched on a cliff overlooking the town and all.

I guided my car up the winding road toward Chamfer's house, wondering what I was doing. I had no plan. My mind was static again.

The gates of Chamfer's mansion were wrought iron, of course. I parked across the street and took a look around. The wood, lodge-style house was situated close to the road, making spying easy. The yard was manicured and pristine. I pulled a small pair of binoculars from my glove box and inspected the property.

Seeing what I wanted to see was a matter of moments, and I pulled away from the curb. The radio, which had grown satirical with recent playlists, favored me with Twisted Sister's "We're Not Gonna Take It." The lane meandered down now, looping back toward town. Main street sliced the town in half, and the library was right in the middle. I swung into the parking lot on a whim.

Microfiche is a dead format, but once in a while the small, rural libraries still have treasure troves of the priceless little spools on hand. I had in mind that I would see what I could dig up on Mr. Arthur Chamfer.

My guts writhed in sour protest. I ignored it and trudged inside. The gray-haired but spry librarian was thrilled to show me the microfiche room and how to work the machine. I found a set of promising spools and set in, my aching belly a secondary concern.

As a DA, Chamfer was a disaster. Keeping Jim Knight out of jail was pretty far down on the list of bad things he did during his "career." He was notorious in at least three counties, and suspected of having a hand in small-time organized crime.

"Chamfer, Considered 'Mob Judge' By Many, Reelected" read one headline.

"Chamfer, Hardesty Accused of Fraud" read another. It was endless.

He only kept his position as DA through a series of bribes, publicity stunts, and intimidation schemes. He got and kept his position as judge the same way. Chamfer was known to have an opioid problem, and suspected in trafficking black market pills.

More than once, the man's secretary found him slumped at his desk from reported "health issues." He claimed several times to have not only health issues, but sleep disorders as well. Anyone paying attention could figure out what was really going on. The evidence was all there. The problem is that the people who spoke out and reported what they knew, regretted it. If they survived.

"How are you doing in here?" The librarian's voice was shrill in the quiet room. I jumped.

"I'm great." I gave her my best nothing-to-see-here smile and she shuffled off.

On the next spool I found a community page from the local paper, dated only a year ago, in which Arthur Chamfer announced his upcoming retirement. When asked what he would do with his free time, he jokingly replied he had enough bourbon and cigars to last the rest of his life, and intended to stay home.

I took pictures with my phone as I went along, to help remember details. I was aware that I was searching for more reasons to go through with my plan; this was different than my chance encounter with Jim Knight. I was carrying out premeditated revenge this time.

After a couple of hours, my entire lower torso was a seething lava pit and I had to leave. But I had what I wanted.

I paid the price for it, too. My stomach was a delicate thing, and how I got home from the library is a blur in large parts. I focused on not letting the pain overwhelm me. Focus was all I had. Pain pills stopped working weeks ago, and I was already fuzzy in the head without them. Medication was out. I still needed to function.

For a little while.

The steps up to my apartment were endless. It took one solid eternity to get my door unlocked and open. The living room was wider than the Serengeti Plain. There was a single moment of bliss as I lay on my bed, right before I passed out both from exhaustion and pain.

My next conscious thought was annoyance at the buzzing sound going off next to my head. Somehow the entire night and half the next day disappeared. It was 1:30 p.m. and I had an hour to get ready and drag my sorry self to the doctor's office. My guts hated me.

I untangled from the sheets and managed a shower and some basic makeup before I needed a rest. I closed the lid on the toilet and sat. The bathtub yawned at me from across the room, and for a second I felt as if I were falling into it. My vision went white, and a soothing feeling spread along my limbs. Something unseen propped me up, preventing me from falling over.

Vision returned and my extremities felt tingly. I considered it might be a stroke, but I had no typical symptoms. I shook myself loose from the weirdness and felt better. Calmer. I had an idea of what happened.

Somehow I got out of the house and presented myself on time to the oncologist's office. Dr. Douglas was annoyed.

"Why did you go on that business trip, knowing your diagnosis?" His eyes pierced me like needles.

"I needed to get away. Process the situation. The trip was already planned and it was a free hotel. If you're worried that I worked too much, don't. I didn't do a damn thing the entire time except order room service and watch free HBO."

He smirked at that, but it did not last long.

"You're not healthy enough to go back to work at all."

My angry belly spasmed in agreement.

Dr. Douglas's eyes were sympathetic. "Look, I'll be frank. We underestimated the growth. Your cancer is advancing at an unprecedented rate. Based on your latest test results, you need aggressive treatment. And you need it now."

I wanted to laugh, but I thought Dr. Douglas might take it wrong so I kept it to myself. He would think I laughed at him, rather than the absurdity of it all. Bless his heart for thinking he could save me.

I made my voice soothing. "Dr. Douglas, there's no need to worry about treatment because I'll be dead by next week."

He blinked, uncomprehending.

"I don't blame you for being surprised. I only found out today, myself."

This had him gobsmacked. He sputtered. "What? What makes you think…?"

"Because."

"That's not a reason." His forehead was like a Picasso: all red, bold lines.

"'Because' is the ultimate reason. Why do some people like yellow, and some people love blue? Because. How come some people love cilantro, and others hate it? Because. Oh, there's always complicated reasons behind everything, but it's easier to simply say 'because.' Red is my favorite color, cilantro is gross, and I'll be dead by next week. Because that's the way it is."

He stared at me for a long time. "You'll definitely be dead by next week if you believe it that firmly. I've seen it happen."

"I believe it like I believe the sun rises tomorrow." He hung his head. "Oh now, don't take it as a defeat."

He gave his head a shake and then lifted it to look at me.

"You're giving up, and I'm not supposed to feel defeated?"

This time a mad giggle escaped. "Dr. Douglas, I'm not giving up. It's just that my time is up, and I have the privilege of knowing it. That's all. I have just enough time and strength left to finish up my task in this life, and then I'm moving on. That's no defeat on your part, Doctor. It's a victory on mine."

He mulled this over. He did not like it much, but accepted it. The remainder of the appointment was spent discussing hospice arrangements and palliative care. I told him I would call when it was time. He wished me well as I left his office, and the light of defeat never left his eye.

It was only 3:45 when I left the oncology wing of the hospital, but I was spent. I decided to spend the weekend resting and making what few plans I needed, and launch my final mission on Monday.

I drove to my apartment, intestines writhing inside me like hot snakes. I stopped by the complex's community laundromat before going home. The place was deserted, smelling of bleach and clean clothes.

The dryers were my target, and I went down the row like a feeding hummingbird. The lint traps yielded a fine harvest, and I stuffed the fluffy wad into my purse. Step One, complete. I slinked out and went home.

Monday morning I repeated my visit to the apartments' laundromat, and scored another big bunch of lint from the weekend. While my neighbors did laundry, I slept and ate what little my worn out belly could take. I returned to my apartment and sat at my kitchen table, where my supplies were spread out.

Black clothes, complete with ski mask and black sneakers. Phillips screwdriver. Aluminum foil. Dryer lint. Rubber gloves. Simple and lightweight, like my plan.

I considered calling my office to explain I was sick, but

decided I did not care enough to make the effort. They tried to call a couple of times during the day, but I ignored the phone.

I ate a few bites of toast and gave up breakfast. My belly was having none of it. Television held little interest but I sat on the couch and stared at it most the morning. It was all terrible. The talk shows and the news, and the circus of junk that passes for entertainment these days. I was not sorry to be leaving all that.

When early afternoon came, I called Dr. Douglas. I was only on hold a few seconds before he picked up the line.

"How are you?"

"I'm hurting, but okay. I think tomorrow I need to see the hospice people, if you can arrange that."

"It can happen today, if that's what you need."

"No, no. Tomorrow is soon enough. I have some things to wrap up first. I want to thank you for all your help."

"I wish you'd reconsider treatment." His voice was urgent.

"It would be wasted effort. But thank you, Doctor."

He told me to expect the hospice nurse at 9:00 a.m. and made it clear I was to call him if I needed anything. Dr. Douglas is a good man.

After that, I napped the afternoon away, waking long after the gray light of evening faded to night. I could feel strength begin to leach out of my body the moment I stood up from my bed. I ignored the unpleasant sensation. I had one last task to complete and I could rest forever.

I dressed in the black shirt, pants, socks, and shoes, then stuffed the mask into a small black purse along with the other items on the table. My wallet went in next, but I left my phone lying on the coffee table.

There was no need to hurry, so I turned on the television. I flipped through the channels, at one point stumbling upon a preacher talking about forgiveness.

I hoped I would be forgiven for my actions. I knew I did not deserve it, but I hoped anyway. Perhaps I should have forgiven Jim Knight. Perhaps I should forgive Arthur Chamfer. But I could not. All I could feel was vengeance. I was broken, and there was no going back.

Offering up a small prayer of forgiveness for what I had done, and was about to do, I turned off the tv and grabbed my purse. I left, the late hour on a weeknight ensuring that all was quiet. I saw no one.

I drove to the bottom of the hill where Chamfer's house stood and considered leaving my car there, but it was too far to walk up the hill in my weak state. I drove on up and risked parking a mere block away, on a small side street. I put on the ski mask.

Street lights were few in the neighborhood, being outside city limits. It was dark as I padded my way up the street to Chamfer's house. The wrought iron fence might have deterred anyone else, but the cancer meant I was scrawny. It was a tight squeeze between the bars, but I managed it without much trouble.

"Please don't let there be a dog." This fervent wish was whispered to the universe as I dragged my rib cage through the iron bars. I did not think of it before that moment, and my senses went alert. I froze just inside the fence.

All remained quiet. No thundering paws coming to investigate met my ears. No barks broke the night. I crept forward, toward the house.

Memories of Jeremy loomed large in my thoughts. He loved science when he was small, and was fascinated by electricity. When he was eleven he did a report on the history of electricity, and begged Jeff to let him rewire our microwave. Jeff said no, Jeremy did it anyway, and that was how our family learned to replace a short-circuited electrical outlet.

I chuckled at the thought. My guts were quiet for once, letting me work.

The towering monstrosity of a house was meant to look like a fancy, five-star resort lodge, all wooden beams and slat siding with thatch covering the roof. Cobblestone paths crisscrossed the yard, and those I avoided. I made my silent way across the grass to the house, following the outside wall until I found what I was looking for. It was almost too easy.

"Bingo." My hand slid across the metal surface I sought.

During my recon mission before, I noted through the binoculars that the house had several outdoor electrical outlets situated around the perimeter. I followed the outside wall around to the back, choosing an outlet near the most private part of the yard. The master bedroom would be nearby.

Finding the outlet I wanted, I removed the outer cover with the screwdriver. I put on the rubber gloves, then removed the outlet from the housing. Conscious that the wires were hot, I gave them a twirl and yank, exposing a short length of bare wire at the back of the receptacle. I let it drop.

The wad of dryer lint came out next, and I stuffed as much as possible around the outside of the plastic housing, and used the rest to line the inside. A small crumpled square of aluminum foil went into the box next, designed to make contact with the exposed wires and arc the outlet.

"Here we go." I shoved the outlet back into the housing. I could hear the faint crackle of sparks as I screwed it back into place and replaced the outer cover as fast as possible. I got lucky again, and everything fell into place just so.

Tiny tendrils of smoke were beginning to escape as I finished up and ran for the fence, sour belly unhappy with the jostling. I scraped my breastbone squeezing back through the fence, but it went unnoticed.

Back at the car, I realized I still wore the rubber gloves when I had trouble opening the door. I yanked them off and jumped in, feeling better, less exposed. I was worn out from the one block sprint to safety. I dragged the mask off my head and smoothed my hair.

To my left, an orange flash bloomed down the street. I rolled the car window down, but nothing came to my ears. No screams or sirens disturbed the night yet. A full five minutes passed in eerie stillness, orange light growing. The glow flashed again, lighting the underside of clouds overhead.

"Someone call 911!"

The voice was faint, not coming from Chamfer's house but the other way up the street. It was enough to rouse the neighborhood. Lights began to snap on in windows all around me. I slouched down in my seat.

A tall figure in a bathrobe came running up the street, still shouting for someone to call 911. He disappeared toward Chamfer's house. The orange glow was bigger and brighter than ever, and the shifting night air brought me the distinctive stench of a house fire. Below the hill, in town, the wail of firetrucks started up. They would arrive soon.

I stretched out across my front seat and closed my eyes. The deed done, my spirit began to ebb away. I dozed off, a light sleep broken by the approach of the fire trucks a few minutes later.

Judging by the size and intensity of the orange glow, most if not all of the structure was a loss. I had no more business here. I cranked up my Buick and pulled slowly out of the side street, inching down the hill into the early morning. "Burning Down the House" by the Talking Heads came on the radio and I burst out laughing.

I watched the rearview mirror like a hawk. Nobody pursued me. I never saw a single police car. It was like every other early Tuesday morning, except for the house burning on the hill behind me.

I drove home, certain now that I was insane. A killer, an arsonist, and nuttier than a five-pound fruitcake. I drove slowly, the pain in my abdomen making it difficult. I had just enough time to shower and settle in before the hospice nurse arrived and I got busy with the business of dying.

***

Confessing all this has wrung the last of the strength from my body. My breathing is labored.

The OSBI agent studies me from his chair in the corner of my bedroom, eyes unreadable. He is here all the way from Oklahoma to catch me. The cancer beat him.

"Do you have children, Agent Holcomb?" He flinches.

"Ma'am, I don't have to imagine what it would be like for something to happen to my child. I was that child."

I am surprised I can still feel sympathy. "I'm sorry." I barely get the words out.

"I remember my parents talking about killing my abuser." He shifts in his seat. "But they only talked about it. They never acted on it."

I do not like his chiding tone.

"Your parents still had something to lose."

He looks thoughtful. "The boy in Jim Knight's motel room was rescued and reunited with his family."

This is the best news I have heard in years. I give Holcomb a smile.

"We didn't know about the arson. I only know about it because the deputy sheriff assigned to me while I'm here was worked up over Chamfer dying in the fire, and I gathered he was a big wig. You didn't have to tell me about that."

He waits patiently while I gather my fading strength.

"Someone needed to know. Someone needed to know about my Jeremy. I'm not sorry those men are dead. I'm not sorry it fell to me to do it. It was wrong, but it's done. And I told you all this to explain myself, not make excuses. There's a difference."

Holcomb's face is conflicted. He reaches for the recording device on my coffee table and turns it off. The hospice nurse comes in to ask if we need anything, and has the good sense to leave when we say no.

She hums "Amazing Grace" as she goes.

"I'll be honest, they'll want to prosecute you for these crimes, despite your illness."

I almost choke on the laughter that wells up. "Go ahead. I'll be dead before it matters."

He nods in acceptance and stands, adjusting the badge and pistol on his belt. He steps closer to my bedside and gazes down at me.

"What you did isn't right, but I understand."

I am too weak for any response but a single grateful tear. Holcomb leaves my room, and I hear him bid farewell to the nurse. The front door closing echoes through the apartment like an empty tomb.

The nurse comes in and gives me a dose of morphine. The pain in my gut fades, and I am drowsy.

I fall into a deep sleep. My first real sleep in months. As I fall further into the blackness, my pain fully subsides and exhaustion lifts. I feel peace, and comfort.

And then I feel nothing.

4. FIRST PLACE LOSER
By PAUL G BUCKNER

The clouds rolled by swiftly, the wings of his P-51 Mustang slicing through the white puffs of cotton like a knife blade through hot butter. The sleek war machine was capable of more than four hundred knots, but today's mission required him to keep the reins held tight, for now anyway. The fighters were to escort the slow-moving, heavy bombers into enemy territory to release their bombs and return home safely. Sounded easy enough, but when a Messerschmitt comes screaming out of the sun with guns blazing, it becomes a bit more of a challenge.

The Mustang pilot had dared to hope the war would be over long before, but May of 1944 found him on another mission deep over enemy lines. Like any young man with any sense of patriotism, he volunteered as soon as his country asked. His grandfather served, his father served, and following in their footsteps, he too, chose to serve, and proudly. He tried not to think about what was about to come, but rather a more pleasant time in his life which was any time before the blasted war. A voice crackled over the radio speakers breaking the silence.

"Nothing but blue skies and white clouds out here boys," the male voice said.

"We're getting close. Keep your eyes peeled," Captain Walters replied.

The Mustangs typically flew in multiples of four per squadron and stacked up in layers around the bombers with the lowest planes a few thousand feet above and behind and the highest layered up to thirty-thousand feet. Enemy fighters would attempt to dive from above the bombers ripping through them before the escorts could track them. They would also mass in huge formations and attack straight on where the heavies were weaker and more vulnerable to attack. It would also minimize exposure of the German aircraft to the massive gunfire of the escorts.

The drone of the Packard Merlin V1650 V-12 engine was comforting; he knew it was faster than anything the Germans put up against him, including the fierce Messerschmitt 109.

The target was a fuel plant located in Ludwigshafen and his ship, which he christened the Comet, cruised at twenty-seven thousand feet, well above the bomb-heavy birds he was protecting. The radio squawked again.

"Bandits at eleven o'clock, low."

The captain's heart raced, pumping hard with adrenaline as they dropped their external tanks and made a tight turn to get up ahead of the bombers. Within seconds bombers in the lead formation were exploding in brilliant flashes of red and orange mixed with thick, black smoke littering the sky as damaged planes spiralled down and flak shells exploded all around. The sound was deafening even through the headsets the pilots all wore. Captain Walters' knees trembled on the pedals in anticipation. Was this the day that he would die? He had survived many skirmishes before, but none of his previous missions were as vital or of the scale as this one. He wore gloves, but he could feel the cold sweat on his palms. Every time he went up could be the last. He knew that. He accepted it. A calm resolve came over him, his steely gray eyes reflected the quiet confidence of a fierce and deadly warrior. After the ME-109's cut through the heavies on their first pass, they headed straight for the escorts, the P-51 Mustangs.

***

The flight was bumpy, hot and muggy, not to mention long. A young Billy Walters tried to sleep, but every time he dozed off, the plane would hit more turbulence and wake him. It wasn't that it scared him, he loved flying, it was merely that the seats were not the most comfortable to be in for long periods of time.

Billy would be competing along with several of his teammates from their mid-western university against some of the nation's best athletes for the next week at the Las Angeles Coliseum. UCLA was favored to take the overall team victory, but Billy was one of two athletes that everyone would be watching. The other, Eric Bergmann, a senior from UCLA, held the title that Billy was there to take away.

The two had met a few months earlier at the 1938 NCAA Cross Country Championship where Billy lost to Eric in an epic battle which was something not many would forget.

Bergmann, a year older and already with a fantastic track record of wins, was only slightly favour

ed over the young midwestern runner who wasn't expected to put up much of a struggle for the senior. To everyone's amazement, once the race started, Billy was stride for stride with the veteran runner. It was even more amazing to Bergmann who thought Walters would eventually fade. Both athletes pushed each other beyond limits they thought possible. In the end, only one was the victor.

The wheels of the plane skidded on the runway and bounced a few times before the pilot was able to land and roll to the terminal.

"Hell of a ride, eh sport," James Perkins said with a slap on Billy's back when they stood to disembark.

"I'll say, Jimmy. It'll be nice to stretch out, that's for sure."

"A few of us are going to get together tonight and tear it up. Jonesy knows a sweet little place swinging 'til dawn. Lotsa cats will be there. I bet ol' Bergmann himself will show up. Maybe you can start getting in his head. You'd like that, eh Billy?" James said grinning from ear to ear. The left side of his face was still red from where he had been sleeping against the window seal.

"Not tonight, I've gotta get some rest. I'm all set for checking into our rooms, getting a shower and getting some sleep. Gotta early morning run planned."

"Suit yourself, buddy, but never say ol' Jimmy Perkins never invited ya," Jimmy said with a laugh.

Once the team picked up their bags at the terminal, they boarded a shuttle and were soon checked into the hotel where they would be staying for the week during the meet.

The men would be staying in a suite across the hall from the women, and the coaches were on the floor just below.

"Lights out at 11 p.m. No exceptions. Got it?" Coach Willerby said.

Several mumbles of assurance weren't much in the way of ensuring compliance at all. The coaches knew some if not all would try to break curfew if they thought that they could get away with it.

Billy followed Jimmy and other men into the suite and found a suitable bed and stowed his gear.

"Okay, fellas, we're gonna scram in fifteen so doll it up and let's beat feet," Jimmy said.

The other men all agreed to the time frame and scrambled to put away their luggage.

"You sure you don't wanna go, Billy boy?"

"No thanks, I wanna keep my head clear and just concentrate on one thing. You boys have fun and stay outta trouble, would ya?" he said, laughing at their excitement.

Billy turned on the radio that sat against the wall and listened to the latest songs for a while. He decided he needed to get some air and maybe a bite to eat to help settle the butterflies in his stomach. He changed clothes, locked the door behind him and took the elevator downstairs. Just as the doors opened, he was met by none other than Eric Bergmann.

"Going somewhere, Champ?" Eric asked.

"Was just going to get a bite," Billy said as the two faced off. "Are you staying here too?"

Eric laughed, "No, no, I stay in the dormitory on campus. I ran into a few of your teammates at the

Bookstore. They told me you were here. I came to find you."

Billy was taken aback by the revelation. Why would his biggest rival be looking for him?

"What do you mean you ran into them at the bookstore?"

Eric laughed again, "Oh dad, haven't you heard? It's only the best joint around. It's just called the *bookstore* for kicks. I hang out there sometimes. Come on, let me show you around town, that is unless you'd rather stay all by your lonesome in the big city. We can grab some dinner on the way."

***

Morning came quickly. Billy had showered, dressed and was out the door before his friends, who had staggered in from their night on the town just a few short hours ago, had stirred. Dressed in sneakers, track shorts, and a gray hoodie, he grabbed a croissant from the hotel lobby and headed to the track at the university for his morning workout. He had a routine and couldn't afford to slack off. He was surprised to see that Bergmann was already there when he arrived.

"Wasn't sure you'd make it or not. Slept in did you?" Eric joked as he continued his early morning stretches seated on the ground.

Billy dropped his duffel and began stretching. "I blame it on the traffic. I've been up for hours. The sun won't catch this fella in bed asleep," he laughed.

"Well, let's get to it before the reporters see us together and start with all the questions and photographs."

The two runners had planned to meet at the track but Bergman, being from the area, knew of a route that would take them out of the stadium and through the campus to avoid all of the reporters covering the meet. Once they had completed their warm-ups, they jogged to the tunnel entrance and out through the parking lot to find the street nearly empty at the early hour.

Over the next few days Billy and Eric spent their mornings working out together and the rest of their time soaking up the warm rays of the California sun on the beach. The two became fast friends based on their love for cross-country running, but they soon found they had other things in common. They may have grown up worlds apart, but they weren't so different after all.

On the day of the race, Billy arrived at the Coliseum accompanied by his entire team and was greeted by several reporters, each of them interested in the what had been touted as *the* race to watch. Bergmann only nodded to Billy when they saw each other. Billy nodded back but made no other gesture acknowledging their new-found friendship. He needed to be in his zone. Butterflies filled his stomach as they always did before a race, but this time was different. He was running against one of the country's best college athletes of all time. Bergmann had never been beaten, but Billy was confident that this would be his day to upset the favorite. He knew that during the last race the two had squared off, Bergmann had given everything he had and only won by a step. The two runners would be putting on quite a show today, and the rest of the field knew they were all running for a third-place finish at best.

Several other events were taking place when the runners were called to their mark, but all eyes were on Billy and Eric Bergmann as they set for the 10km run.

He barely glanced at Bergmann when the two shook hands and exchanged, "Good luck." Billy's butterflies suddenly disappeared as they always did. He loved the feeling he got just before the starter's pistol fired. It was one of resolve, confidence. His face was drawn taught, emotionless in stark contrast to his loose and lithe body as he warmed up and stretched one last time before stepping into the blocks. He planned to ease out and settle into his own pace, keeping his stride consistent. He would run his own race and keep the rhythm he had worked on and not be pulled into running against anyone and being yanked away from his strategy. If he were able to stick to his game plan, he would be running stride for stride against Bergmann in the end. That's when he would make his final move.

The two stars lined up on opposite ends as Bergmann drew the inside line. The noise of the crowd faded away, and Billy was left with nothing but his own thoughts. A sudden smile flashed briefly across his face. He was in the zone and felt good. He was sharp, loose and ready to do battle.

The starter's pistol fired, and the runners shot out of the blocks, each one trying to get to the front of the pack and move to the inside as quickly as possible. Bergmann was quick and found his way running smoothly toward the front of the group with Billy not far behind. Within the first lap, Billy had settled in comfortably behind his rival and locked into his pace trying not to be influenced by the others.

Two laps later, the two runners began to pull away from the rest of the field and eventually had gained more than a hundred meters of separation. Halfway through, Billy found himself only three steps behind Bergmann. His lungs were clear, and he felt good as he watched the footsteps of his friend and rival. Billy wanted this win today more than anything, but Bergmann wasn't going to just give it to him. It would be a fight all the way down to the wire.

Billy focused on his internal clock as he began making his move on Bergmann. His rival was strong and wouldn't allow himself to be outpaced. Bergmann was prideful and wanted to win dramatically. Billy planned to take that away from him and put Bergmann off his game by pulling ahead even for a short time. It could unsettle his opponent just enough to knock him off his game and get in his head. Billy's strides lengthened ever so slightly and within moments was stride for stride and even. He chanced a glance at Bergmann and thought he saw a hint of a grimace. Perhaps his plan was working as he kicked ahead to lead by a couple of steps and forced his rival to step up.

The starter signaled the start of the last lap with a bell as Billy and Bergmann passed him more than half a track length ahead of the nearest runner. Billy still lead by two steps. His lungs burned from the brutal pace. He knew he had to keep something in reserve for this last lap but was concerned he had spent it on leading. But if he was hurting, so was Bergmann.

Billy heard the footsteps and labored breathing of his rival as the UCLA star slowly gained the few steps back and paced him. Side by side the runners came out of the last turn heading for the finish line. The crowd was on their feet watching the spectacular race and getting the show of a lifetime between the two All-American athletes. Billy Walters and Erik Bergmann were stride for stride and breaking for the finish line, giving everything of themselves, leaving nothing on the table. Only grit and determination kept their legs churning as their bodies burned every ounce of energy and screamed for more.

***

When the German fighters finished their first pass working over the lead formation, they headed straight for Billy's squad of fighters. Billy, flying lead, sent his birds into a sweeping left turn to engage the bandits even though it exposed their bellies to the enemy.

"Bandits at five o'clock," Billy's wingman called out.

Four Messerschmitt's screamed straight for the Mustang drivers hoping to take them out with a quick pass before returning to wreak more havoc on the heavy bombers.

Billy reversed his turn and pulled hard right to go nose to nose with the ME-109's, allowing his squad to pull into a string formation. The German pilots broke away with amazing agility after the pass. The Mustangs banked hard making a one-hundred-eighty degree turn and give chase. Billy expected the Germans would be making another strafing run on the heavies he was there to protect, but instead of heading for the formation, the ME-109 pilots turned to engage the Americans.

"Looks like they wanna play fellas. Let's give 'em hell," Billy said calmly into his radio.

This isn't what these guys usually do, Billy thought.

For the German pilots to come after the escorts was rare. They usually went after the slow-moving bombers to take out as many as they could before heavy payloads could be dropped on strategic targets. They would avoid a battle with the escorts, but this group was different. Billy sensed it.

The Mustangs banked hard and fell in behind the ME's all in a straight line flying in a tight concentric circle, like vultures waiting on the spoiled remains of another's kill. The German pilots were at full throttle, but the Mustang's more powerful engine allowed the American drivers to gain quickly on their tails. They would soon be lined up perfectly to open fire.

Four American pilots flying P-51 Mustangs chasing four Germans in ME-109's in an aerial dance was a preamble to a dogfight through the very gates of hell, like two boxers squaring off. The tension was as thick as the black smoke from the downed bombers.

The German pilots, knowing they were outgunned, rolled out of the turn and banked straight away for home, but the Mustang drivers weren't about to let them off easy and gave chase, making sure it wasn't a trick of some kind.

***

Billy's legs burned like they were on fire searching, screaming for more fuel that just wasn't there. His knees threatened to buckle beneath him as he pushed his body harder than he ever had just to stay even with his rival. Bergmann too struggled. It was only a matter of who could maintain the brutal pace another twenty meters. Billy focused on the finish line.

Was that a stutter step, Billy wondered? *Did Bergmann falter?* His concentration broken, he found himself thinking about his own legs, his focus on the finish line suddenly averted to his own feet.

Heavy. Uncontrollable. Can't put them down evenly. Just a few more steps. Almost there.

The entire stadium was on their feet, and the cheers were deafening as the runners crossed the finish line. Both men spent every ounce of energy, will, and determination, then collapsed in a heap just a couple of meters beyond the finish line. Eric Bergmann was the winner by two steps.

Billy Walters entered the small coffee shop in the hotel lobby and sat at the bar.

"Coffee please, black."

"Sure thing sweety," the waitress said. She turned a cup up and filled it with the hot steaming brew from behind the counter then turned away to see to another customer at the other end.

"Mind if I join ya, Champ?"

"I'm no champ," Billy said as he turned to the newcomer.

Eric Bergmann sat down on the barstool next to Billy and put a hand on his shoulder.

"You are in my book," Eric said. "I called your room several times. I figured you were brooding."

"Brooding? Yeah, I guess I kinda have at that," Billy said. Disappointment clear in his voice.

"Let me tell you something Billy boy, you have nothing to brood about. We are both winners here. This is my last year, and you're just starting your track career with one of the best performances of a lifetime. We both set track records ya know?"

"No, I didn't know," Billy said, turning to him.

"Oh yeah. That was one race that will be remembered for a long time to come."

"Yeah, maybe. So, what are you going to do now? I'm sure you have job offers lined up."

"Yeah, I do, but my parents want me to move back home, join the military. They said I could be an officer. I dunno. They paid for my college so I guess I owe them," Eric said. His voice changed from the normally robust and energy filled to a trace of melancholy. "I'm going to put them off for as long as I can though. With any luck, it'll be a few years," he laughed.

The two men sat and talked most of the morning before heading out to grab some lunch. For the next few years, the men would exchange letters and postcards and get together when they could. Good friends became best friends built on competition and school rivalry, but turned into a genuine kinship. Billy liked the fact that Eric never once gloated over beating him. Never once had he offered anything but encouragement. The take away from the rivalry, for Billy, was never losing focus, don't let others distract you from choosing your own path.

One day, the letters stopped coming. Billy wrote several more times but no word. He hoped nothing bad had befallen his friend, but he knew his friend had lamented about following his parent's wishes and joining the military.

Before Billy could graduate, the war had found its way into the lives of people all over the world. He and several friends joined the military. He had always wanted to be a pilot, but not necessarily for this reason.

***

The Mustangs closed the gap in the iron circle above the clouds, and Captain Bill Walters lined an ME-109 up in his sites and squeezed the trigger. Immediately the German plane puffed out a tremendous cloud of black smoke with flames scorching the gray paint and turning it coal black. The flying steel wasn't going down easily so Captain Walters hammered it again. Finally, the plane exploded in a tremendous fireball and began a tumultuous descent spiraling down through the clouds on its way to the ground more than twenty-thousand feet below.

Another Messerschmitt pilot suddenly broke away in a sharp climbing turn banking hard and maneuvering swiftly to cover the other pilot's escape by attempting to separate the Mustangs and drop in behind.

Captain Walters sees it and goes after the German plane which now seemingly wants to fight, but is obviously covering for his wingman's retreat. The Captain swung his aircraft in another steep bank and rolled into a sweeping turn to line up for a high angle shot, but the German pilot anticipated the maneuver and pulled hard to pass in front of Walters and flew right by.

"Dammit, Bucky! This guy is good," Bill called out to his wingman.

"You're telling me," Bucky said with a strained voice as he hauled on his rudders but was unable to keep up.

"I think I took some flack. Steering isn't responding. It's tight," Bucky shouted over the radio.

"Head for the deck, and I'll cover you, Bucky boy," Billy replied.

"Good luck, Cap'n,' Bucky replied dropping his nose and turning. He knew he was a sitting duck and would be more of a hindrance than a help in the dogfight.

One of the German pilots saw the Mustang break away and arced his plane in a tight loop to give chase. Billy spotted it and reversed his direction to go after it. He dropped in perfectly for a snapshot, but just as he started to squeeze the trigger on his guns, the Germain pilot pulled out in another turn causing Billy to overshoot and fly right by allowing the German to pop in right behind Billy's Mustang.

Dammit, almost had the bastard. Billy thought. *You're good, buddy. Really good. Another perfect reversal. It'll not happen again.*

Billy pulled hard and headed for more altitude with the Messerschmitt hot on his tail. He knew he had to keep his nose up and simply outfly the German. The Mustang was faster and had a higher climb rate than the 109.

"Come on, stall out you bastard," Billy shouted. He knew they only had seconds before one or both planes would stall and then fall like bricks. Whoever stalled first, would surely be a goner. Maximum throttle at a vertical climb, neither war machine could hold out much longer. Billy's plane began to shudder and shook violently.

"Come on baby, just a little longer," Billy coaxed his Mustang as he looked back over his shoulder watching the 109. His engine screamed like a banshee, defying the force of gravity.

The 109 wobbled and suddenly stalled, halting in mid-air as if held suspended in slow motion. Billy saw it and immediately flipped the Mustang over and spiraled down on the German pilot. Lining up the gun sites, he squeezed the trigger, but the 109 wasn't giving up. Rounding out of the dive, the German found enough power to maneuver his plane out of the stall and re-engage with Billy's Mustang.

"Dammit!" Billy shouted. "Almost had you!"

The Captain tried to turn in front of the 109 taking a huge chance by exposing himself if only for a split second. He would lose a lot of airspeed in the turn, but if he was successful, he would have a clear shot. To keep his power up and maintain as much speed as the plane could muster, he dropped his flaps and tightened his turn radius. The aircraft shuddered under strain but held the line dropping in perfectly for the shot, but the 109 suddenly snapped away into another vertical climb.

"Not this time," Billy said through gritted teeth.

When the ME-109 pulled straight, he exposed his belly for the split-second Billy needed. The machine guns spit out a fury of cold steel into the German plane. It immediately puffed smoke and pummeled out of control, falling for the ground far below. He knew it wasn't a ploy and the plane was going down for sure when he saw the prop stop and twist inward toward the nose cone. With a huge sigh of relief, he followed it down as far as he could before his low fuel forced him to turn.

The 109 pilot was the best Billy had ever come up against. With a quiet salute, Captain Bill Walters turned for home, grateful for one more day. His tenacity and focus kept him alive.

The war ended in Europe with the unconditional surrender of Germany in May of 1945. Japan would hold out a little longer and not sign a surrender until September 2nd. The Japanese surrender came after the United States dropped the atomic bombs on Hiroshima and Nagasaki in August.

***

"The Colonel is expecting you, sir," the secretary said as she stood and held the door to the office behind her reception desk.

Bill Walters stood tall and firm, his lean figure dutifully held erect in his olive-green flight suit. His short-cropped salt and pepper hair and thick mustache gave him the appearance more of a cowboy than a fighter pilot. Several years had gone by since the ending of the war. Bill Walters, an ace fighter pilot from WWII, now a test pilot flying jets for the military, was set to retire in a few short weeks.

"Please come in, Captain Walters," Colonel Pratt said as the secretary held the door open. "Have a seat."

"Thank you, Colonel, and thank you for seeing me. I know this was a difficult request, but after the war, I often wondered about that German pilot. He was good, really good. As an instructor, I used his moves for training."

The Colonel's expression changed to a more stoic look as he stood and strode to a file cabinet in the corner and opened a drawer. After a moment of shuffling through files, he pulled the one he needed and returned to his desk. The old wooden chair groaned and squeaked under the weight.

"I bet you'd be surprised to know that it's not nearly as odd as you might expect. I don't know if it's from regret, respect or whatever the reasons may be for each person, but I get it. It wasn't easy to get this information, but we got lucky."

The Colonel pushed the file across the desk.

"It appears the 109 driver that you shot down was an ace, having been credited with several downed enemy pilots. Germany lost one of their best when they sent him up against your squad. By shooting him down, you probably saved a lot of lives."

Billy listened to the Colonel before picking up the folder. He tried ignoring the manilla file laying in front of him, but his mind raced in anticipation.

"I'm grateful for that at least, Colonel. It was war sure, but I wouldn't ever wish a man dead, not unless…well, you know, it had to be."

"Of course, I understand."

"He was just the best pilot I had ever seen. Some of those moves are part of today's curriculum for young pilots, as a matter of fact."

When Billy opened the file, he read the entire contents of it never hearing another word that the Colonel spoke. The color drained from his face. He only looked up when he had finished every word. The Colonel was standing over him with a hand on his shoulder.

"Captain? Captain Walters?" The Colonel jostled him. "What is it? Are you okay?"

"The pilot…I didn't know…never knew, though I guess I must've…should have anyway," Bill stammered as his shoulders trembled.

The Colonel could see Bill was apparently distraught. Overcome with grief for the taking of another's life or was it something more?

"What is it, Captain? What's in there?"

It took Bill a moment to collect his thoughts and composure before replying.

"His name was Eric Bergmann, and he was my best friend."

5. INSEPARABLE

By AARIKA COPELAND

I sip the sour coffee. It does little to calm my nerves. Neither can the sludge tame the ever-shifting thoughts in my mind. Like sand dunes, the memories slowly build from the pit of my whiskey filled stomach. Rising till I feel the grains grind between my teeth. Until they drown out the sound in my ears. But I sip, heat from the brew scalding my tongue and helping me to focus.

I roll my shoulders. Force my arms to relax. A wetness glides across my free hand dangling at my side. I look down. See Ray licking my palm, searching me with those amber eyes.

"You doing alright, Ronin?" Buck asks me. "Haven't shared yet. Anything on your mind?"

Lots of things. "No."

I lift my hand away from the German Shepherd. Focus on the circle of veterans surrounding me as Ray lies back down behind my chair.

Mike sits to my left. His left eyebrow ticks in tandem with his tapping foot. If that don't speak to his anxiety, the neck and hairline boils will. Demetri is to Mike's left. His salt and pepper mustache mirror the curtain of silver hair smooth against his neck. Impassive. Unimpressed. A veteran of being a veteran. Karen's to the left of Demetri. Cropped copper hair with long bangs that cover up those vacant, sunken eyes. Unconcerned hands folded listless in her lap. She looks through me, to beyond the doorway. And then there's Buck. Crinkles deep in the bronze skin around his eyes as his cracked lips quirk up in a small knowing smile. An 'I get it' smile.

Not one of us is crazy. That's not why we're here. Regret is a driving force. If you don't handle it, it'll steer your life. But it ain't regret of our service—we would all die for the common good. Maybe pieces of us have. We're here cause' the regret of the things we couldn't do, the lives we couldn't save.

Buck lets the silence stretch. A quiet invitation. He won't allow me to dismiss group discussion. Won't keep me from trying each time. When Buck flares his nostrils in impatience and I simply blink in response, Buck takes the lead.

"Come on, Ronin. How's that wife?"

Shit, Sheila.

I look down at my coffee. At the lumps of powdered creamer yet to dissolve. "You know," I suck my teeth, "my wife likes the finer things in life." I rub the four-day stubble on my chin, leaning back in the chair until the polyester creaks. "Guess that's why she's in our lawyer's bed tonight."

No one makes a move to speak. The silence ignites a fire in my thoughts, eager to devour every morsel of my mind. Ray sits up, staring expectantly at me. Her nails clicking against the linoleum. I ignore my furry companion and continue.

"I ain't mad," I say. "Truth is, I lost Sheila before I lost my leg." I shift in my seat, an ache running through the phantom limb of my left leg. "Can't rightly blame her. I knew she was as shallow as the short end of the swimming pool. But damn, did she look good in that lace dress."

This elicits a few terse laughs. Even Karen ain't immune to my jest; the ghost of a smile forming in the corners of her lips before they flatten out to their normal line. My lips pull into a smile too. I down the rest of the caffeinated ooze, the black liquid ineffective against the onslaught of dark memories.

Sheila failed to answer my Facetime request. For the second month. I was often behind enemy lines. Part of a forward observation base unit. The only chance to communicate is in the cybercafé on the air base. She hadn't answered.

Misshapen dinosaur drawings and a prayer of protection. The only mail I received that day. From my sister and nephew back in the States.

I looked forward to those crayon drawings. But the impact of Sheila's absence hit me hard. Shrapnel to the chest. I was gone too long. I knew. I prayed to be with her soon. I needed to get home.

My prayer was answered the following day.

"Sorry to hear that, Ronin," Buck says, yanking me back from the recesses of my thought. Back to the too bright room and a sour churning belly. "But I see you got yourself a new friend." He gestures to Ray.

"We're getting to know each other," is all I say, ignoring the service dog. None of the other thoughts I've had toward the dog will get me out of here any faster.

"Seems like it."

I follow Buck's eyes down toward Ray who has inconspicuously placed her paw on my artificial thigh.

Karen makes the first exit after the meeting. She keeps to herself mostly. Shares the least in the group. Even less than me. Don't blame her. I wouldn't talk much either.

Karen served alongside her husband. Brother, too. Karen was the only one to come home.

Grief is a tectonic shift. The collision of two losses, it fractures deeper than the eye can see.

Karen and her daughter are my neighbors, but there ain't nothing neighborly about our acquaintance. We keep to ourselves. Both too miserable to do much more than survive.

Buck and Demetri make themselves available after the meeting. Nursing coffee from paper cups and nodding along with either Mike's ticking eyebrow or his words. "We've all suffered," Mike says. "And I guess we're all just trying to get back to some sort of normal." I don't feel like sticking around to hear the rest.

I start through the door, forgetting Ray, but she's quickly brushing against my right leg.

Outside the VA, Ray's tongue lulls in the July heat. She matches my hobbled pace. Resentment flairs, knowing she's slowing to keep near me. I extend my stride. But she's there. Inseparable to my needs.

I pull my shades on. Move us toward my parked truck. I don't mind the warmth. The sun shines differently in the States. Softer. After two nine-month tours in Iraq, my skin absorbs the heat with ease.

Opening the door, Ray jumps in and moves to the passenger seat.

"Back. Go on. Get."

She looks at me, giving a small whine. Ray's tongue drips on the seat. I'm bout' to grab her scruff when she decides to jump to the back seat.

I lumber up into my seat. Turn the ignition. Feel the

truck thunder to life and rev beneath me. I pause. Despite the number of times I get into this truck, the flare of the engine's potential power is a loop to the past. A place I spend my days trying to forget.

Ray prods me with her nose, a tether to the present. My fingers find the button. Pressing down so she gets a bit of airflow.

The clock on the dashboard reads 1:15.

Shit. I ain't got time to take Ray back to the trailer. Tasha, Ray's trainer, said she don't do well on her own. Needs the constant companionship, or something. Taking her to class is different than group. But I can't afford to skip another class.

I shift into gear, Ray falling against the back seat before eagerly tossing her head out the window.

It's a ten minute drive to campus and I'm veering into a spot with four minutes to spare until class begins. My left leg aches under the transfer of weight it takes to ease myself out of the truck. Grabbing my pack from the passenger seat, I begin to shut the door when Ray whines.

Double shit. I can't leave her in here.

"Let's go," I say, patting my leg. Ray obeys the command, jumping over the center console into the front seat before hopping down. She hugs close to my right leg, giving my hand a quick lick.

"Alright, enough. I'm good. Just," I pause as a pair of students walks past. When they're out of earshot, I continue. "Listen, I'll keep it together if you do. No funny business while we're in here, got it?"

Ray's ears work. Listening, but already focused ahead. "Gotta hand it to you pooch, you'd make a decent sentry dog."

I shut the door and we're off toward Spencer Hall.

Sunbeams ricochet off the windows, cutting into my

vision despite the glasses. Imploding buildings. Shower of ruble. Tinkle of glass falling like rain. Discharge of lightning and fire. The heavy scent of baked earth and gunpowder in my nose. A barrage of noise. A quiet whimper.

Ray nudges my fiber leg and whines. I don't feel it. Not in any physical way. But her nose cleanses the thoughts. I push her away in annoyance. Frustrated with being the one to lose it first.

I start up the steps to the front door, having to hold the rail to center my balance. She stays next to me. Her eyes constantly darting up. Alert. Waiting for her next command. Waiting for another to slip in time.

My Economics class is inconveniently located on the second story of Spencer Hall. Once I'm up the steps and inside, I'm met with a brief blast of cool reprieve before the inside staircase taunts me with the next challenge. The stairs are a bitch to hike up with this bum leg. It's one reason I've missed so many classes.

The sound of clicking keyboards greets me as I move toward the first step. I glance in classrooms as I pass. Students cushioned and softened as the padding on their computer chairs. Unaware. Disconnected.

I used to want to be a big shot accountant. Working billion dollar contracts. Make loads of money. Be able to tip servers a hundred dollars. Buy a bunch of worthless shit just because I could. All obtained from the seat of a chair.

I'm medically retired now. Incapable of work. I'm reduced to a percent of income on a spreadsheet. I can't help but formulate myself as an expense.

Those dreams belonged to a whole man. They were torn from me and left to decay on foreign soil with my lost leg.

Elongating my left thigh, I stretch out the ache and start up the stairs. Both legs burn as I make my ascent.

My jaw is a vice when I reach the classroom. My lungs

work through my nose. My back beads with sweat. Ray and I try to slip into the room unnoticed, but her clicking nails and happy grin pull eyes toward us. A flush creeps up my neck.

Mr. Littlefield begins to protest, his white eyebrows dart upward and his belly pushing out. But the bright color of Ray's vest cuts him short. I'm the one who feels like the animal though, as he cuts his eyes to me next. Tail tucked. A snarl toying on my lips. I look away and lead Ray to the closest chair.

I sit and wave a hand behind the chair. A command for Ray to settle at my back. I don't like admitting it, but Ray is a comfort here. The certainty of someone having my back is an instant calm.

Most people don't understand the value, what it means having a soldier at your back. I was never alone in combat. Strangers I'd only known a few weeks became brothers and sisters. We protected one another. We fought for each other. That protection ain't an easy thing to let go of or forget. Not when the lurking shadow of an enemy threat decides to stay.

Faces gradually turn back toward the front of the room and the lesson begins. I manage a few notes. Suddenly my throat is dry. I'd give anything for a cup of water. Hell, I'd even take that sludge they call coffee from group right now. Mr. Littlefield's words are white noise.

Bang.

The air unit kicks on and jumpstarts my pulse. Throat tightening. My muscles automatically tense as I scan for exits and threats. Four windows line the wall to my left. No latches. Would need to be busted out in case of emergency. Ray shifts. Snapping my head around, I check the open door.

Ray rises her head. She makes a noise in her throat, but I

silently give her the command to heel. She obeys, worry twitching across her eyebrows.

Mr. Littlefield's words hum like an aftershock in my ears. Maybe he isn't even speaking. Maybe, I think between burning swallows, that buzz, that acoustic whomp in my skull, is a breach in my mind.

Not today. I squeeze my eyes closed, knotting a fist against my temples. Someone scoots a chair across the floor. The sound like the crunch of sand below boots. No. Dammit, I think, kneading my fist deeper into my forehead. Shit's going wrong.

With that thought I've launched away from the classroom, ripping through space and time, only to land back in hell.

"Shit goes wrong, it's all of our lives on the line. Keep it tight. Keep your eyes open." My unit hunkers around Gunnery Sergeant Gibson as he explains strategic maneuvers, preparing us for the next rendezvous check.

Each of us eager to see pockets of green again. Buzzing with energy to keep pushing further. Thin clouds cap the mountains in the distance.

"With a high priority target, you wanna send three down range," Sergeant Gibson scans a map, his finger following across as he speaks, but he looks up to meet our eyes as he says it. Each of us stares back. "That goes for your personal lives too." He says it so quickly, I barely have time to grasp his words before he dives back into his assessment of our mission. "Prior proper planning prevents piss poor performance."

Planned and prepped, we load up the Humvees. It's all our lives on the line.

The roads are clear. Haven't made unfriendly contact in almost two weeks. Don't matter. We keep our eyes on the horizon and our ears trained to listen past the whir of engines and the pulse of life in our ears. Every nerve on end, our muscles tight as the grip on our rifle.

My breath quickens, and I ain't sure if it's just the anxiety or a primal fear it might be your last.

As the Humvee bounces across alien desert, my mind soars across oceans and land. I'm hundreds of miles away. Wrapped in the thought of my wife's arms, her kiss on my neck. A prayer on my lips to see her soon. I am lost in her embrace when the IED takes out the first two Humvees in our squad.

Bang!

I'm on my feet. The chair pushed out from behind me. Ray skids along the linoleum in panic. My chest heaves and my mind races to catch up. Faces stare at me, shock and confusion in their eyes. My body's slick with sweat despite the chilled room. Room. I'm in a classroom.

"Sorry," I croak. The word almost splits my throat. Ray nudges my hand with her nose. I absently stroke her head. I grab my pack from the ground and lead us out the door.

In the parking lot, Mike's words from group repeat back to me.

We're all just trying to get back to some sort of normal.

As I move my carbon fiber leg across the pavement, I wonder, how the hell do you find normal? How the fuck can you find north when your new north is the moment you want to forget?

Ray seems agitated, overtly alert. Her tail slightly tucked. A whine between each chance to lick my hand. And I allow it, a sorry for frightening her.

"We're going home," I tell her as I open the truck's door for her to leap into. "You must be sorry you got paired with me, huh." I wring my hands, working against the tremor running through them. "Listen, I get it if this ain't working out. I probably don't got no business with you anyway. There ain't much worth salvaging here."

The wind shifts. The scent of the campus cafeteria reaches me. My stomach responds to the smell of fryer grease, but I know I won't be able to eat even if I try. Ray seems to catch it too, because she's poking her head out the open door, her long nose moving against the breeze. I'm reminded of Ray's empty food bowl at home. "Alright, we got one stop. But then we're going home."

I reach for the ignition switch once I'm settled in the front seat, but fall short, a violent tremor coursing through my hand. I feel a pressure against the top of my shoulder, where Ray has laid her head. I reach up to push her away, but my shaking hand finds the fur between her ears instead. The tremors eventually even to a slight tremble as I stroke her ears. We stay this way for a long moment.

Ray's head is still against mine as we pull onto the road.

My chest tightens as the grocery store enters my line of sight. Among the pulse of bodies hide faces and voices of my dead. The illusion of their presence clutching at me like a vice. Coward, I curse myself. It still takes thirty minutes for my hand to find the door handle.

Ray jumps out and hugs my leg, her head actively rubbing against me. "I'm fine," I hiss, but Ray continues her investigation. I pat her head to placate her, but my chest eases a bit instead. My thoughts shrinking to the softness of her fur. "We'll get through this."

I take a cart from the greeter standing just inside the automated doors. Her gaze shifts down to Ray, then to my left leg. She quickly averts her eyes and mumbles something that sounds like 'good day' as she rushes to help the next customer.

Ray stays close while we navigate the aisles through the rove of carts and people who wander around recklessly. We go to the pet aisle first and load the shopping cart with a bag of dry dog food. I add a few wet cans of food that Ray might appreciate later.

The liquor aisle passes in my peripheral and I tow the cart around, heading back to hook a bottle of Jack. Envy for the man I once was flares inside me at the sight of the brown liquid. I never used to have trouble sleeping. Sheila used to joke about my ability to sleep anywhere.

After I came back to the States, the VA doc prescribed sleeping pills. But I quickly realized that shit traces into my waking world. The nightmares digging trenches for me to trip into. Jack Daniels works better. It drowns the dreams before my mind fully breathes life into them.

Ray and I scout the frozen dinner aisle next. Waving a hand behind me, Ray settles on the floor at my back. I do my best to control my eyes and mind to each immediate task, like, which questionable meat dunked in sauce pairs best with alcohol. But an unexpected face strikes my attention.

Karen wears a green vest with the grocery store's logo over her heart, her back hunched slightly, her arms limp against her sides. An image of her straight-backed, donned in laced boots and tactical gear flares in my mind's eye.

Though she's only a few feet away, she doesn't notice me. She stares intently at the freezer doors, and I can almost see her mind working as she looks through the glass. Her eyes searching shelves for the unattainable.

She turns to me then, recognition dawns. A single nod, voicing her pain in the gesture. Our eyes hold for only a moment before she turns, leaving us both to continue our broken paths.

I feel the need to say something, do something, but before I can form a thought a voice interrupts. "Hey, is that, like, a trained dog?" The voice throws me a moment. I don't see who spoke at first. But I find a young boy squatting in front of me, staring at Ray.

"Yeah. She's a service dog. Name's Ray."

The boy can't be older than nine. Coppered skin like Buck. Cropped hair. Lanky. All bones.

"Hey, Ray," the boy says. "Can I pet her?" He asks, looking up to me.

"Sure." And I can almost see Ray puff up a bit, hold her head higher so the boy can pat her and rub her ears, but she stays on her belly, continuing her command.

The boy looks up to me again, taking in my buzzed hair and the peek of an American flag tattoo just below my shirt sleeve. "Are you a soldier?"

"I am. I was," I correct myself.

"You're a veteran?" the boy asks, having finished with Ray's pets and standing.

"Yeah."

To my astonishment, the boy thrusts a hand to me. "Thank you for your service, mister," he says.

I'm so dumbfounded I leave him holding his hand out for a moment. I regain my sense and clasp it, giving him a good pump. A smile forms in the corner of my lip.

"Gramps told me I need to say that when I meet someone who helps protect our country." The boy looks borderline embarrassed by the transaction, but generational pride squares his shoulders in a way I understand.

"Your gramps sounds like a good man. My grandfather served. Did your gramps?" The question brightens the boys face.

"Yes, sir. Served twenty years. Retired a Master Sergeant." And I can see the swell of pride in the young boy's chest when he says it.

"He your hero?"

"Yes, sir. You're someone's hero too, I bet."

The smile fades from my face.

I think back to the first week I spent in the field hospital after I lost my leg. Medics working beneath yellow lamp lights. In my drug-induced state, they morphed with the tent flaps whipping in the wind. Desert monsters that clawed at me with scalpel fingernails and chewed my heart with their needle-like teeth. The chant of hero on the monsters' lips. Dust and dirt coating everything, the land inescapable. I waited, hoping the sand would bury me and the name of 'hero' forever.

"They called me a hero. But I never felt like one."

Truth is, I was just getting credit others deserved.

"Did they call you hero cause' you lost your leg?" The question spurs another smile. No one has ever asked me so bluntly about my leg, and this boy asks without judgment. Only a sense of gratitude and curiosity.

I'm about to answer when a woman rushes toward us. "I'm so sorry. He just thinks everyone is willing to tell their story to him." The woman glances down at my leg, at Ray, and I can see a flush creep over the tips of her ears and splotches form on her cheeks. She rushes the boy away, the boy waving me a goodbye as they turn the aisle.

I abandon the frozen dinners and head to checkout.

Standing in line I try to shut my eyes, cut off my surroundings, but it's against my instincts. I can stomach the quick glances, the darting eyes to Ray and my prosthetic leg. What is deafening are the tormenting tunes of strangers as they unload their grocery carts onto the conveyor belt. Complaints of potholes. Unfair prices of hamburger meat and soda. Of friends who aren't showing up to their perfectly planned Fourth of July party.

I wonder what they'd say if I told them their right to bitch is built upon pillars of bone and flesh, not colored coordinated plastic cups. That blood is the cement of their nation's foundation.

Shit. It ain't me who needs change. It's the world.

I know Ray senses my frustration as she begins her prodding. I reaffirm her by placing my hand on her head and stroking her ears.

My lungs expand once we're outside. The vice loosened from my chest. Even the rumble of the truck doesn't do its normal trick. I shift into gear and put as much pavement between me and that damn store as I'm able.

Sheila left me when the disability checks couldn't cover the mortgage. Now I rent a thirty-foot-long trailer squatting in disrepair at the end of a horseshoe-shaped mobile home park. I sold most of our belongings in an estate sale because I don't need much anymore. But I couldn't let go of my Grandfather's Smith and Wesson revolver, or the pair of walkie-talkies my dad had bought my sister and me when we were kids. The money went into a savings account—an investment from one appreciative uncle to his dinosaur drawing nephew.

Ray hops out of the truck when I hold the door for her after parking on the grassy patch of earth next to the mobile home. She heels at my feet while I haul out the bag of dog food, slinging it over my shoulder, the bag with the bottle of Jack and canned food in my other hand. Ray keeps close, but she relaxes the physical contact as we walk up the mildewed wooden steps to the door. Dusk crowning the trees and clouds in a pale orange.

I fumble with the keys when the first round of pops go off in the distance. I figure this Fourth of July can't beat last year's when I was bedridden. When the sounds of fireworks had burst through my memories, ripping my reality asunder.

But as my hand tremor starts again, I'm not so sure today will be any better.

Ray notices and begins her incessant prodding. "Dammit

dog, get off me." I manage to slip the key into the lock and turn the handle. Ray and I all but tumbling in as the door swings open. The bag of dog food tips off my shoulder and I'm forced to let it fall to the ground. The paper rips open as it hits, food scattering along the linoleum flooring.

"Fuck! Come on. I need you out of the way. Let's go!" I grab Ray's scruff and lead her to one of the bedrooms. I grind my jaw at her obedience to follow. She stares at me with those molten eyes. I close the door hard.

Back in the connecting kitchen and living room, I take stock of the mess, the sound of "Free Bird" now vibrating through the tin walls. Cheers of drunken party goers shout their love of the U.S.A. outside my window, flanked by the sound of those damned fireworks. Pop. With each blast, I'm back in that desert. Pop. Blood in the sand. My dead squad scattered around me as indifferent as the kibble at my feet. Pop.

I leave the mess. Find the bottle of Jack. Planting myself in the recliner.

I've spent months masking the pain, but with each burning swallow of the whiskey, pop, my mind shakes loose images that have danced in my peripheral all day. Thick and heavy. Swimming in amber currents of time and reality. Memories of misfortune and death. Pop. Another two gulps. Pop. And the thoughts take hold.

The world tumbles and jolts. Screams rise above the ringing in my ears. Thick clouds of black smoke camouflage the scene beyond the Humvee window. I don't want it to clear.

Outside the Humvee, blood and fuel soak the sand crimson and black. Steaming metal and tire, the smell of fire and flesh. The stench seeps into my nose and settles bitterly on my tongue. The pop of gunfire, the whizz of bullets. My eyes pinpoint charred remains a few yards away.

Who is it? Captain? He rode in that first Humvee. My body reacts while my mind rushes to catch up. I turn away and regroup.

My team forms a link, ready to assist the fallen. We make our way to the front of the rubble. Bullets cutting the air near our heads, forcing us to hunker near the ground and maneuver around the rubble. Myself and another close up the rear. Jensen is his name. Young. Clumsy. Overwhelmed with the cries for help and the gunfire ahead. He trips over a strip of tire. I snatch his arm to keep him upright before he impales himself onto a slice of burning metal. That split second saves our lives, but not my leg.

Another IED explodes, sailing us backward. The midday sky bursts into a white haze. My body numb as I impact the ground. My thoughts flee to my unit. Their bodies ripped across the desert from a single burst. I try to pull myself up. I try to roll. Pain seizes me. The quiet in my ears too enveloping. The pop of bullets breaks the barrier, but not enough to rouse me. I blink against the dust clouds, and the world slowly collapses. Darkness takes me.

When I come to, blood coats my tongue. Smoke and hot metal fill my nose. Sand whips across my eyes and sweeps down my throat forcing a heaving cough that burns my lungs. My eardrums are busted, committing me to land of silent horror. Ash floats on the scorched breeze. Beyond the shroud of smoke, blue sky peeks through. Swirls of white clouds pushing past.

I'm not sure how long I lie here in limbo, body useless, until faces swim into view. Yelling voiceless words. I'm injured, that much I gather. But pain is a distant thought. It won't come until months later.

My finger twitches and I'm momentarily startled. My grandfather's revolver in my hand. The weight of it in my palm is reassuring, familiar and steadies the tremor. I rub my thumb along the engraving on the barrel. Captain Billy Walters.

My finger twitches again, eager to play soldier. Alone in this trailer, there's only one enemy. And I don't think he'll fight for his life.

I steady my hand, placing the handgun down in my lap, but not letting go as I take another swig of Jack.

Each burst of fireworks solidify the shadows clinging to the corners of the dimly lit trailer. Familiar faces form. Watching me through empty eyes.

 I close my eyes and let the world fade to muted gray. My breathing heightens and mixes with the quickened beat of my heart. I wonder if the machinery in my lap just might be a key.

The barrel is cold against my temple. A rush trills through me. More than I've felt in days. My thumb finds the hammer. I pull back. My breath hitches when I hear the click, like a key unlocking some sealed secret only privy to the shadows. The world narrows until it fits entirely inside the circumference of the revolver's barrel.

I wish I hadn't saved Jensen. I wish I had been shredded to oblivion.

The barrel digs deeper with each thunderous burst of light from outside, the trigger in full reach.

Bang!

My eyes fly open at the sound. Bang, bang. Someone pounds at the front door.

I close my eyes and dig the barrel harder against my skin. Bang!

"Hey Ronin, you in there?" calls a small voice. I pull the pistol away quickly.

"Uh . . . one sec," I say, blinking. Hastily assessing what I had just been about to do. It wasn't real. But the revolver firmly in my grasp disagrees. I shuffle out of my chair and move to the front door. Ray's frantic barking comes from the back room. She starts scratching at the floorboards. Or had she always been doing it?

I turn the lock and pull open the door just enough to see who it is while concealing the revolver behind my back.

Two people stand on the wooden porch outside my trailer. A young girl with the same auburn hair as her mother standing next to her. Karen.

"Hi!" The girl waves, a smile across her face. "We're having a party, wanna come?"

I look at Karen. Her smile is almost genuine. Until she takes in my appearance and likely picks up the scent of whiskey on my breath.

"Sorry. Didn't mean to bother you Ronin. This is Ashley." She places a hand on Ashley's shoulder. "As she said, we're having a party, and she wanted to invite you."

"Thanks, but I'm no fan of the fourth," I say, my voice coming out a bit slurred. I attest this is more from the uncomfortable situation than the booze.

"Good," Karen replies, "because it's Ashley's birthday party."

"Yeah, we're eating cake and hitting a peenata." Karen smiles down at her daughter as Ashley mispronounces the word, and I feel my lip twist up too.

"I'll save you a piece of cake if you don't wanna come, but I think you should," Ashley says before running down the three wooden steps. She stops at the bottom and turns back toward me. "Bring your dog! I'll give her some cake too." Ashley bolts across the lot to their trailer, leaving Karen and me alone.

Karen keeps a trained eye on her daughter until she's safely back home, then turns toward me.

"I understand if you don't want to come over," she sighs. "Truth is, it hasn't been easy planning for this party.

I've dreaded it for weeks. I thought I'd fall apart. First birthday without her dad. But now that it's here . . ."

Karen looks across the lot, and I follow her gaze to where Ashley dances around a picnic table, her pigtails flying as she spins.

Karen looks back at me, the faintest smile on her lips. "This, this thing we have," she gestures to her head without entirely focusing on me. "It's not easy, and sometimes the bad days win." Karen looks at me then. "But it's not about living above it, or below it, but side by side. It's the only way to move forward."

Karen offers a nod and turns to leave.

"Wait," I say before I even know what comes next. I look behind the door at the firearm in my hand. I lower the hammer.

I let Ray out of the room, where she is still digging at the floor. She rubs against me, licking my hands and makes an offensive sound in her throat. I tuck the revolver into the waist of my pants before kneeling to rub Ray's head and ears.

"Sorry, girl. We got a long way to go." Ray reaches up and works her tongue eagerly over my cheek. "Alright. Alright." I hear the chuckle in my voice and Ray must too, cause her tail starts swaying. "I ain't gonna leave you like that." And I know it's true, cause Ray won't leave me. "Our neighbors got a treat. You want a treat, girl?"

I grab Ray's food bowl from the kitchen and scoop up some of the littered dog food from the floor. Karen is still waiting at the front door when Ray and I step out together.

Acknowledgments
The completion of this story could not have been possible

without the following service members:

John D Ketcher Jr., who offered encouragement and direction in the creation of Inseparable.

Jon W. Ketcher, I appreciate your help and insight. Thank you for being candid in your experiences.

To Spanky Gibson. Your thoughts and actions helped form the most powerful statements in Inseparable. I thank you for your willingness to allow me into your past.

Jared Johnson for affirming my accuracy in this story.

To Juan Luna. A constant symbol of perseverance and loyalty.

To my dad, Carlos Ochoa, for teaching me awareness and how to not just plan, but act, to ensure my future.

6. FAMILIAR

By AARIKA COPELAND

Tree limbs rose above them and spun across the sky. Web-like shadows stretched over the paved walkway between the late evening rays.

"You're sure this is where we are supposed to meet her?" Everett kept his eyes trained on the cement line ahead of them.

"Yeah, this is the address," Tasha answered. "She said she would be waiting on the bench facing the water."

"I don't think I've ever been to this park, or have even seen it, for that matter," Everett said, his eyes roving over the spindly trees.

Everett's comment twisted uneasiness around Tasha's mind, and she had not intended to confirm her concern, but the words passed over her lips. "Me either. None of this is familiar."

She swallowed and looked over her shoulder to the wrought-iron gates of the entrance behind them, then to the cracked and pummelled blacktop where their Jeep sat. A two-headed street lamp illuminated from behind the browned leaves of a lone tree gave the tree the impression of glowing eyes that tracked Tasha and Everett's movements.

"You haven't brought the dogs to this park?" Everett asked.

The word no stuck in Tasha's throat as she faced forward, turning her head away from the entrance and those glowing eyes. She had started her dog walking business only a few months ago at the start of summer to earn extra cash. She enjoyed the long walks with her canine clients and did her best to switch up the scenery for them. She drove all across town to walk the dogs in every park or trail she could find. But she'd never seen this park before and had not read about it in any online searches or local trail and park maps she had purchased.

Preyer's Park. That's what the sign said, or she guessed anyway. The last half of the faded and splintered letters had been scratched away, leaving only the legible word Prey.

She refused to let Everett know the extent of her unease. It must be newly renovated, she decided. She wrapped her sweaty palm around his hand and started forward.

It was twilight, and a bruise hung over the skyline.

Meet me before the sun sets. I don't do well at night.

Tasha reiterated to Everett what the woman said on the phone earlier that day, the memory of those words now slid a chill down her spine. She chalked it up to deep pity. The thought of a slow, frail body and an ailing mind a concept she rather not ponder. But the question gnawed its way to the forefront of her mind now. Why would this woman want to meet in the late evening when she opposed the night? In a park nonetheless, where lighting was poor.

"Well, we better hurry then," Everett said. "Night is closing in fast. Let's find this lady. Water, you said?"

Tasha nodded and they both hurried their steps.

Lamp posts lazily flickered to life as they passed beneath them, the sudden hymn of electricity following close behind. The mountains in the distance cut a jagged line across the sky as the sun sank below their peaks, leaving only a bloody cut out of their form. Tasha watched as the last red rays fell away. Darkness cast its cloak over the park. The street lamps, seemingly more illuminated, began to attract eager swarms of bugs. Other than Tasha and Everett's heavy breaths and quick footfalls against the pavement, the only sound of life was the gentle pings of the bugs' bodies as they kamikazed into the bulbs.

Tasha didn't mind walking in the dark. She often took her clients' dogs on late evening runs. Especially when their owners were out of town. It calmed them and burned off enough energy to keep them from being restless in the night. It often did the same for Tasha.

But not tonight. The silence only made her more aware of their seclusion. The path only seemed to go forward. She didn't see another jogger or cyclist around, and night really was falling. It clung to every curve of tree trunk and blade of grass.

Her stomach swam in doubt. Should they turn back? Don't be ridiculous, she thought. She'd waited weeks to meet Mrs. Nichols. If she turned back now, she'd likely have to wait another year for this opportunity. But how could she ignore the shivers tiptoeing across her body, goosebumps of alarm?

But then she heard it. They shared knowing glances just as the eerie atmosphere was about to get the better of Tasha. There, barely audible above the writhing of insects was the gentle babble of water over stone.

Everett's teeth flashed yellow in the low lamplight. He pulled Tasha along with long strides.

Everett should be the dogwalker, Tasha thought. His long legs could keep up with the endurance of her four-legged friends more easily than Tasha's. She had often invited Everett to accompany her on their walks, and even offered to split the payment, but Everett always said no. "I'm a cat person," he'd say, looking down at the leashed animals with accusing, pinched black eyes.

She didn't share his love for their feline counterparts. Cats were pretentious snobs. They also decorated your house in hair. Everett's admiration for felines was the reason they were here in the first place. At Prey park. At night. Alone.

Or maybe not. As they moved forward, their steps echoing out like a harbinger, a shadow slinked into Tasha's peripheral vision. Everett maintained his march, but Tasha slowed, pulling her hand from Everett's. She strained her eyes through the darkness to her right. She roved over the outlines pressed into the night so intently, it sent an ache shooting behind her eyes. The night remained still. Had she imagined the movement?

She started forward, but it came then, gliding along like a shadow in between tree trunks. A low, guttural growl vibrated the night. Tasha stiffened. Her temples pooled with cold sweat. Its outline stalked closer—gaunt, four long legs, a protruding rib cage, and narrow torso, and, God, needle-like spines jutting from its back.

"Everett." The word came out like a squeak. Relieved to have formed any words at all, she tried again. "Everett!"

Everett stopped a yard away and turned back. Annoyance flashed across his raised brows. Tasha lost her ability to speak again and pointed past the walkway, to where the creature roamed. Everett followed to where she pointed. They both searched the darkened landscape, and when they didn't see anything, Everett turned to her.

"Are you alright? Do we need to leave? You're freaki-"

A loud bang cut him off. Tasha skidded across the walkway in a panic right into Everett's arms. Instinctively wrapping her in a protective embrace, she felt Everett shivering with fear. She tucked her head into his chest. After a moment she realized he wasn't shaking with terror. No.

He was … laughing.

Tasha looked up to see a playful smile on his lips. He gestured to Tasha's right, back to the location of the beast. Tasha craned her neck to see. Lying on the ground, just beyond the weak light of the lamps, laid an overturned trash can. Poking out of its gaping pit of a mouth was the bushy tail of a scavenging raccoon.

Tasha pressed against Everett and exhaled, a twitch at her lip pulling into a smile. Her imagination had never proved so creative before, and she shook her head at her folly.

"You alright to keep going?" Everett rubbed the unease from Tasha's back, his mouth trying to hide the smile from a moment ago.

"Yeah." She shook off the anxiety. "Yeah, I'm fine." She gave her best smile, which seemed to convince Everett, but when Everett looked away and started back down the path Tasha cut her eyes to the raccoon. She swallowed hard. Why did it stick in her throat though? Why did her intestines continue to writhe in her belly?

A few minutes of walking and the sound of water became louder. Everett noticed the bench first. It sat beneath a triangle of yellow light. The glow from a nearby lamppost illuminated a lone figure.

They found her. So, why did Tasha feel like the night was creeping in, holding them prisoner in their spot? Everett gave her a side glance and Tasha couldn't muster the fake smile this time. Concern carved its way around her eyes and mouth and Everett mirrored the look.

"Mrs. Nichols?" Everett's words came out thick. Heavy. Like he was speaking from far away.

Tasha gripped her hand around Everett's arm as they both inched forward. They came closer. Close enough to make out the outline of the woman sitting on the wooden bench. The rush of water echoed louder than the hum of electricity now. A shawl wrapped tightly around the woman's head. Her small figure sat straight. Too straight. Rigid.

"This place is giving me the creeps," Tasha whispered, clutching Everett's arm tighter.

Everett tried again. "Mrs. Nichols? You spoke to my girlfriend on the phone earlier. You said to meet you here? We're sorry if you've been waiting."

Everett slowed his pace but continued forward. A flickering sound came from behind them. Tasha turned to see the lamp lights fighting off the darkness, winking in and out. One by one, the darkness triumphed. Like a wave of a hand, each bulb burned out. All but one. The lone light shining above the woman on the bench.

"I think I'm starting to get that bad feeling too, babe," Everett whispered, leaning into Tasha.

They inched closer, Tasha craning her neck in every direction. Standing only a few feet behind the bench now, but Mrs. Nichols still hadn't acknowledged their presence. Everett pulled Tasha's hand from his arm and stepped away from her.

"Mrs. Nichols?"

Everett reached out a hand. It hovered midair. Then, he placed it on the woman's shoulder. He jerked his hand back like he'd been burned.

"What is it?" Tasha shrieked.

Everett snaked out his hand and ripped the shawl from the woman's head. Tasha gasped at Everett's audacity but sucked in a harsh breath when she noticed the smooth plastic of a mannequin's bald head.

The rush of water through the creek and the blood in her ears filled the world. Everett stepped away from the dummy, joining Tasha back beneath the center triangle of light. They stared back down the dark path they just traversed when a movement caught Tasha's eye. She heard the growl then.

Low. Hungry.

A snap of a twig forced her closer to Everett, and she felt his body tense against her. She could hear it moving beyond their line of sight. Everett's eyes bulged with an effort toward the sound.

Something rushed past them, leaves and twigs turned over in its wake. Tasha lept back and Everett hugged her closer. Tasha burrowed her face against Everett's chest but looked up when he whispered against her head. "Do you see that?"

She looked up just in time to see a figure emerge from behind a nearby tree. It wasn't the predator Tasha saw earlier, but a human outline. Someone watching them. Realizing they had been spotted, the person moved out from behind the trunk.

Limping, the person made their way forward. They could run back to the Jeep, but they couldn't see. Why hadn't she brought her pack? Tasha thought of the flashlight and pepper spray tucked safely away in her Jeep.

A voice pierced the silence, creaking like an old floorboard. Terse. Icy. "You're late."

The person drew closer. Tasha and Everett backed away to the edge of light as the person stepped into the beam. The yellowing light contoured the old woman's face into a grim horror. Hollow. Wrinkled. Bloodshot eyes. She looked like a corpse came alive.

"Mrs. Nichols?" Tasha said, her voice wavering.

"Yes. You're late."

Tasha let out a low sigh and eased away from Everett, but Everett refused to let go.

"Y-yes," Tasha answered, exchanging a glance at Everett.

"See you met Alice," Mrs. Nichols said, eyeing them both through her round spectacles. "My trusty diversion. Never can be too careful. It's why I don't like meeting in the dark. Bad things happen in the dark."

Everett peered down at Tasha in question as Mrs. Nichols continued. "So, you enjoy the feline divine?"

"Actually, I'm a dog person."

Mrs. Nichols cut her eyes to slits, her steely stare penetrating. Tasha quickly continued, "Everett is the cat lover." Mrs. Nichols' eyes opened and she beamed at Everett.

"Yeah. I'm a cat person," Everett said, forcing his eyes away from Tasha's, still suspicious of the entire exchange.

Mrs. Nichols' smile was a wicked thing: aged teeth made browned by the shadow of her lip, wrinkles drawn like an old curtain around her mouth.

"Well then, you'll love Tabby."

Mrs. Nichols reached in the pocket of the oversized bathrobe she wore and pulled out a bundle of cloth. She pulled the blanket back to reveal the face of an orange tabby kitten.

"You take good care of her," she said, holding the kitten out to Everett. "And remember, she still bites."

Everett's shoulders relaxed and he unlocked his grip on Tasha, taking the bundle in his arms. The kitten purred inside the blanket. Everett scratched under its tiny chin and gave a sheepish smile to Tasha. She understood. She too felt foolish over the entire ordeal.

Tasha looked up at Mrs. Nichols to thank her, but she was gone. She scanned the park, but she was nowhere to be seen. Even the dummy had vanished.

"Where the hell did she go?" Tasha asked, panic rising in her chest.

"Hmm?" Everett offered, still entranced by the bundle in his arms.

"Let's get the hell outta this place!"

Everett walked out of the light and back down the dark path, still comforting the small purring kitten. The lampposts hummed and illuminated once more as Everett walked past them. Tasha took longer strides to keep up with him.

They made it back to the Jeep in one piece, and Tasha was happy to put Preyer park behind them. Settled behind the safety of her locked Jeep door, Tasha asked, "Is she perfect?"

"Absolutely!"

Tasha reached out a hand to pet the kitten's head, but it hissed as Tasha drew near.

"It's alright, kitty. I'm nice."

Tasha leaned in for a stroke of its head when the tiny kitten lurched forward and latched onto her finger. "Damn! It drew blood," Tasha hissed, pulling back. A warmth slid down her finger and began to gather in a small pool on her palm.

"It's not an it," Everett scolded, not bothering to investigate Tasha's bloodied hand. The kitten's back arched as it hissed again at Tasha, its spine rising against flesh. Its tongue glided over its nose, red with Tasha's blood. "Her name is Tabby," Everett said, stroking Tabby's protruding vertebrates. "And she must be hungry."

7. INVITATION
By JULIE JONES

My tiny salon sits on an awkward triangle of land, wedged between an overpass and a concrete noise reduction wall. A lovely neighborhood sprawls across the acres on the other side, but I have been here so long the residents ignore me. My old, black cinder block building with the neon red hand in the window are a forgotten part of the scenery.

I stay because I have no reason to be anywhere else. I am accepted here, and these days, left alone for the most part. When I opened my salon thirty years ago, the novelty of a medium in the area drew customers. My uncanny accuracy drew crowds.

The crowds thinned, over time. Skepticism replaced hope in the hearts of my customers. Technology surged, making people more interested in the scientific than the psychic. Even my regulars faded, either losing interest over the years or passing away.

Still, every few months I find myself entertaining a group of ladies enjoying a girls' night out. I give them the highlight reel of what I see, and do my best to guide them without influencing too much. They leave with lighthearted promises to come back soon, and a fun story to tell around the office Monday morning. I am a party trick, an anecdote.

Only the truly desperate seek me out now. It is those searching for serious answers that I am wary of. An inexperienced medium can wreck lives; an expert can destroy them.

It was late November when I felt a shift in the pattern that meant change coming. Dusk gathered itself into dense clumps of shadow as I descended the stairs to open for the night. The creaking's of the old staircase were muffled by red velvet carpet, flowing down in a bloody tide to spread wall to wall throughout the first floor. Thick purple brocade curtains, heavy with gold tassels, framed the windows.

"You are my favorite." These loving words were for my Monet, hanging on the wall above the fireplace.

Polished mahogany gleamed everywhere in the low light. Atop a rich, antique Persian rug in front of the lobby fireplace sat a small, gold velvet sofa. The matching coffee table waited for tea service.

Since my strategy of the last fifty years or so was hiding in plain sight, a round table, flanked by chairs and topped with the quintessential crystal ball dominated my reading room, visible through the doorway on the left. A heavily padded wingback chair with side table sat in the corner near my bookshelves.

Typical of the season, the sky outside was gloomy and blustery, hustling the evening toward darkness. I was glad to have my thick blue wool shawl and roaring fire. The neon red hand went on in the window, yellow eyeball in the palm blinking to life. I swished my skirt away from the curtains and unlocked the door.

"Good evening, Jeremy."

Brow furrowed, he floated anxiously around the lobby, not bothering to manifest his legs. Mist from the hips down, he made circles that were both lazy and agitated.

"Are you upset about something?"

He paused his circuit to give me a concerned look.

"Someone is coming tonight. She will need answers. Real ones, this time."

I thought about this as I lit a candle. "She is not the first to need real answers."

"No, but she has been Touched."

I paused my evening opening ritual. "How deeply has she been affected?"

Jeremy sighed. It was a flimsy, wispy sound like wind blowing lace curtains. "I don't know. I won't know until she gets here. But it must be deep for me to expect her."

"Will Jeff be joining us?"

"Yes, dad's coming."

I nodded at this and continued with my routine, glad to know my spirit friends would be in attendance. I could manage alone, but guides are helpful. Being Touched means that at some point, a person was given a glimpse of the future that was life-altering, usually not for the best.

Dealing with someone who has been Touched is tricky. The roots grow depending on each person's temperament, age, impressionability, vulnerability...so many factors even I could not catalog them all. Those unlucky enough to be Touched young are often lost.

I lit more candles and a stick of slow-burn incense, then made a pot of tea. The tea I wanted. The incense I only bother with because, much like the crystal ball, in this age it seems to be a required element of visiting a medium. My customers are disappointed if it is absent. Jeremy coughed.

"That's fake. Spirits don't cough."

He gave a wry twist of his lips. "No, but I remember. All

the drug dens I hung out in before I got clean had incense going constantly. They thought it would fool the cops, I guess."

Jeremy floated into my salon four years ago, sad and confused. A former addict, he was killed by his dealer for debts owed just as he started getting his life together. He needed someone to talk to, a willing ear to help him work through his anger at dying so young. I was happy to oblige.

"Do you regret those days?"

"Of course I do. But regret only has power if I refuse to learn from it."

I smiled at that.

Spirits often visit the earthly domain, but despite the number of ghost stories that circulate, few remain in one place for long. They come for every reason. Some seek absolution, some plot for vengeance, some watch over their progeny. From time to time through the long years, a spirit finds me and stays. Jeremy, and later his father Jeff, were two such souls.

I did not ask them why they sought out my company, and I never tried to keep them with me. Only evil can bind a soul to earth against its will, and I am not evil. Spirits are harder to read than the living, but I knew they were waiting for something. My salon provided a comfortable refuge to them, and I enjoyed their presence.

The evening stretched out. Jeremy continued his silent patrol of the lobby while I settled in my reading room with a book. Around 10:00 p.m. I felt a shift in local pressure and knew Jeff had arrived. He floated through the outside wall, coming to a stop in front of my chair. Jeremy joined us.

"Hello everyone." Jeff's brown hair was characteristically disheveled, and his eyes held a familiar twinkle, though it was brighter than ever that night.

"Hi Dad." Jeremy floated to his father and they embraced, sending a warm, pleasant ripple through the room's atmosphere. I greeted my friend.

"Good evening, Jeff. I see you've received some news."

He was surprised, despite being used to my abilities.

"Yes, indeed." He turned to Jeremy with a smile, taking in the younger man's expectant face. "Son, it's almost time."

"Mom's coming home?"

"Soon. Very soon. These last weeks will be her most difficult, but she is coming home."

My eyes would have misted, if I were the sort to do so. I might have been, once. I do not remember. The men, being spirits incapable of corporeal tears, had dry cheeks as well. But their souls were full. The vibrations in the room thrummed with their happiness.

So this was what they waited for.

The front door swung open, the small chime hung above it tinkling a warning. I left the jubilant spirits in the reading room and went to greet my customer.

Red hair framed a flat, pale face dusted with freckles. Tall and well-dressed, she appeared forty, but was not. Exhaustion and worry painted her features, but tension leached away from her body as she closed the door and came further into the lobby. The joyous vibrations emanating from the reading room were too strong for even the blindest Third Eye to miss.

I extended my energy outward, feeling the shape of her aura and confirming what I already knew. She was Touched. My connection fluttered a painful note, then broke. The joy coming from the other room subsided like water draining out of a bathtub.

"Good evening. How may I help you?"

Her brows reknit themselves into lines of worry. "Hi.

Uh, I was wanting to talk to you, if I can. If you have time. I don't have an appointment or anything. I just sort of did this on impulse, you know? So if I need an appointment, that's okay, I understand. I was just driving by and I saw your red hand with the eye on the palm, so I turned in the parking lot. It's so weird. I've lived here my whole life and I don't remember ever seeing this place before."

I drew my fringed shawl close around my shoulders and let her ramble. Mortals do that when anxious, and I have all the time in the world.

"It was so nice, coming in here. It felt so happy and peaceful. It's gone now, but it felt nice for a minute there. I hope that means I'm in the right place."

I gave her a smile. "You are. Come in."

Her shoulders relaxed a fraction, and I gestured for her to accompany me to the reading room. Fresh tea sat on the table waiting for us. The boys were thoughtful that way. They hovered in a corner, watching the proceedings with keen interest.

When she was settled in with her cup, I began.

"So Diane, you have questions for me. I am ready."

She froze at my correct use of her name, tea cup poised for a sip. People never know what to make of that, despite it being the easiest thing about them to read. It inspires both awe and trust in my ability, and when dealing with the Touched, both are necessary.

Diane recovered herself and took a shaky drink of her tea. She returned the cup to the table as if she did not trust her own hands.

"I don't really have specific questions. I just came in totally on impulse. I can think of some questions if you want. I'm great at thinking of questions."

"Let me ask something, instead. Have you had a psychic reading before?"

"No."

"Are you sure?"

She looked thoughtful. "No, not really. I mean, one time when I was a kid, some old lady looked at my hand and told me some stuff, but nothing like this."

I felt my eyes sharpen like a raptor's gaze. "What was her name? Do you remember what she said?"

"Uhhhhh...Mrs. Park, I think? It was forever ago. She told me I wouldn't have my own children. And she said I'd have a hard life full of sadness, and lose my husband early. I guess she's been mostly right, now that I think about it."

I knew the name. Loretta Park was a local school teacher with limited and undeveloped skills. Those like her are known to those like me. People like Park are born with bare glimmers of my abilities. Many of them live and die without any great harm given or received. But occasionally one like Loretta Park comes along, just strong enough to ruin lives, careless of the influence her words might have.

Few things in this world are more dangerous than a doomsayer with a success rate.

"Ah, Loretta Park. So she's the one that Touched you?"

Diane's cheeks flushed pink. "Well, no, ah...not like that. She just looked at my palm for a few minutes, that's all. Looking at the lines and such."

I gave her a disarming smile. "What I mean is, what she said to you that day Touched you, didn't it? It became the fundamental narrative of your life. The underlying theme. Am I correct?"

She turned this idea over in her mind, and did not seem to like it.

"I don't know."

"Why did she not say you would find love?"

Diane blinked in confusion. "What do you mean?"

"If she saw that your husband would die young, why did

126

she tell you that? Why that, instead of saying that you would find love? One gives you hope, the other does not. Am I correct?"

Long pause. "I mean, I guess."

"Do you believe in yourself?"

"Huh?" Confusion was strong in her voice. I repeated the question.

Diane scooted forward in her chair, preparation for flight. "I believe in myself, yeah. But she was right about a lot of stuff."

"You don't believe in yourself. You believe in what Loretta Park told you twenty years ago."

I was blunt, and she flinched at my flat delivery.

"Maybe this was a mistake."

"The truth is never a mistake, Diane."

"How do you know my name?"

"The same way you knew to turn your car into my parking lot."

This caught her short, and she did not answer. She teetered on the edge of her chair, undecided if she should fly.

Jeff made a small noise from the corner, and I swung my gaze in his direction. Jeremy was nowhere to be seen. Diane's eyes followed mine, but she saw nothing.

"She's looking for something. Something that belonged to her husband. Jeremy is seeking the answer for us."

I tipped Jeff a nod of thanks, then locked eyes with her. "What is the object you're looking for?"

"What's in that corner? What were you looking at?"

"My spirit companion. He said you're looking for something."

Diane slumped into the chair. All the wind left her sails. Her face crumpled into fresh mourning, doubling the amount of lines.

127

"It's so silly. A keychain. A Batman keychain. He carried it for a long time, but it was getting worn out so he put it up somewhere. It was his favorite memento of us. He had some important papers I need too, but I'm desperate for the keychain. That sounds dumb, doesn't it?"

"Not at all. Don't worry. I can help."

She dissolved into tears. I pulled a lace-edged handkerchief from my sleeve and gave it to her, then sat back to wait. There was no hurry. She needed the catharsis, and Jeremy needed time to find our answer. Jeff kept still in his corner, eyes sorrowful.

Her tears were winding down when Jeremy returned. He gave me his findings, then retreated to the corner to join his father. I turned to the sniffling Diane.

"There's a room on the back of the house that your husband added two years ago. He built a secret space under the floor. If you move the couch and pull back the carpet, you'll find it. There's a fireproof box inside with everything you're looking for."

She stared at me in dumbstruck amazement, tear-streaked cheeks shiny.

"You can't be serious."

"I am. That's where it is."

She scrubbed her cheeks with her hands. Mascara smeared around her eyes, but I saw a light of hope bloom.

"I have to go home and look."

"Of course."

Diane fumbled with her purse, reaching inside for her wallet. "What do I owe you?"

"First time customers receive complimentary readings."

She stared at me. "Complimentary? You mean free?"

"That is another interpretation, yes."

"If that box really is under the floor, can I come back and tell you about it?"

"Please do."

Behind Diane I saw the front door open. A hunched figure in an oversized bathrobe darted across the lobby and past the stairs, toward my tiny kitchen in back. Diane beamed at me, lighter of heart than when she came in, and stood to leave.

"I really will come tell you if that box was there."

"Yes, Diane. I will see you soon."

She left in a swirl of cold autumn air. I returned to my reading room, settling in my wingback chair with a book. Soon, the doorway darkened with a familiar figure.

"Hello, Mrs. Nichols."

"Hello." Her voice sounded like sandpaper.

"You've been out delivering a familiar this evening?"

"You know that's what I've been doing, so why ask like it's a question?"

I chuckled. Mrs. Nichols did not find the humor. Her glasses glinted at me with annoyance, then turned to my spirit friends. She let out a small hiss.

Jeff and Jeremy remained in the corner, ramrod straight and full apparition. I could see the individual threads on Jeff's shoelaces. Manifestation on that level is the spiritual equivalent of a threat. They did not like Mrs. Nichols, and she felt much the same about them.

"Play nice, children."

They were reluctant, but the boys turned down their intensity, and Mrs. Nichols subsided. The tension level in the room dropped. She slithered closer to my chair.

"You're plotting something." She sounded too interested.

"I am contemplating."

Mrs. Nichols fastened me with a look. "Plotting."

"I suppose that is another interpretation, yes."

Her battered face smirked. She eyed the two in the

corner. "Do they have to be here?"

"They are my friends. They are welcome any time, for as long as they wish."

Jeff cut in. "We can leave, if you want. Not happily, but we will go."

Jeremy mumbled agreement.

"Nobody goes anywhere unless they wish to go. As long as we all behave, I will not order anyone to leave. Is this clear?"

The three agreed and I stood, leading Mrs. Nichols to the lobby for tea by the fireplace. Jeff and Jeremy came along, maintaining distance between themselves and our visitor, taking up guard duty behind me on the sofa.

"What is this thing you plot?" She remained forward as ever.

"I plot nothing. I am considering extending an invitation."

Mrs. Nichols blinked, eyes like smoldering coals behind her round glasses.

"You want me to help?"

"I appreciate your offer, but I can handle it."

She grunted at me. I maintained outward calm, careful not to let her see how much I did not want her involvement. Her people are clever, but mercurial and unpredictable as well. She was a useful friend to have in some situations, just not this one.

Mrs. NIchols gave me a brief rundown of her recent happenings, right up to that evening when she left a kitten with a young couple at Preyer Park. She showed up every few weeks, drank a pot of tea and told me what she was up to, then disappeared again. It was her way, and I never questioned it.

She kept close watch on Jeff and Jeremy throughout the account, but they never moved from their place behind me.

She left soon after, claiming a late-night appointment. Jeremy and Jeff relaxed when she was gone, finally retreating back to their usual half-manifested state, mist from the waist down.

The hour grew late and I felt there would be no more business or visitors for the evening, so I locked the door, turned off the neon hand, and blew out most of the candles. I left a few burning in my reading room, and settled into my wingback chair.

Closing my eyes, I extended my aura, much as I had when Diane came in earlier that evening. This time I focused all my thoughts into one tiny flame, concentrating on the dancing fire. When I was at one with the flickering light, I reached out to search.

I searched the threads that our souls weave to make the pattern of life. Each one was a living person, twined into the tapestry. I skimmed the shining strands, looking for a particular one. I narrowed down where she might be in the pattern, and at last I found her.

Loretta Park's life thread was long, over ninety years. Long, but still vibrant. I studied it, noting the major themes of her lifetime, taking in details about her as I went. I was saddened by how often the bright, promising life threads of others contacted hers in the pattern, and went away from hers so much dimmer.

Carefully, delicately, I feathered Loretta Park's thread with my presence. It was subtle. Just the lightest pressure of my aura, like brushing someone's elbow on a train. I retreated, pulling away from the pattern to return to the flame, and myself. She would not know what compelled her to seek me out, but she would.

Satisfied with my evening's work, I read by candlelight for an hour before bidding Jeremy and Jeff goodnight.

Diane appeared five days later, early in the evening. I

came downstairs to open only minutes before, dressed in my customary skirt and shawl. The candles were lit, but no tea was brewed. Through the front window I saw her park her car and get out. She rang the front bell at the same moment I opened the door.

"Good evening."

"It was there!" She beamed at me.

I gave her a smile in return and stepped aside, gesturing her to enter. She bustled in, and I led her to the sitting place by the fire.

"It was all there, exactly like you said!" She caught her toe on a leg of the coffee table and almost fell, collapsing onto the gold sofa with a laugh. "Look!"

She thrust her hand toward me, keys clenched in her fist. A faded, worn Batman keychain dangled from the ring. Her face was joyous.

"I found a bunch of old war medals, too. I think they belonged to my husband's grandpa. They all said 'Bill Walters' on them. He was crazy about his grandpa. I'll probably give them to his sister because they were all pretty close."

"That is wonderful, Diane. You found the papers you needed, as well?"

"Yes! Yes, now I can turn in his life insurance claims and pay my bills. I can't thank you enough. What can I do for you?"

I smiled at that. "Just keep surviving, Diane."

She shook her head. "No, I need to give you some money or something. What's your normal rate?"

"Typically I ask fifty dollars for thirty minutes."

She furrowed her brow. "That seems cheap. Not that you're cheap. Just that the price seems low. Like, you could totally ask more than that and people would pay it. Are you kidding me? You told me where to look for the one thing I was desperate to find. I was here a lot less than thirty minutes and it was worth a lot more than fifty bucks."

Diane pulled her wallet out, searching the contents.

"Here's two hundred." She put a pile of twenties on the coffee table. "It still seems pathetic considering what you did for me, but it's better than fifty."

Her mind was set, so I accepted payment with a gracious nod.

"I can't stay, but I promised to come by and tell you if I found the box. And I wanted to pay you. I felt bad the other day, not paying for your time or your obviously awesome advice. So I'm glad to stop by and let you know."

"Thank you, Diane. I'm glad everything worked out."

"Me too."

She left, assuring me on her way out that she would stop in sometime, but I knew I would not see her again. In our brief acquaintance, I gave her new things to think over and contemplate, and if I did it correctly, she would flourish without me.

When Diane was gone, I made a fresh pot of tea and sat on the gold couch in the lobby. The universe is many things, but random and coincidental are not among them. People use the word "coincidence" when they cannot, or will not, see the deeper workings of existence. I did not wait long.

Bells tinkled and the door swung open. A wizened, elderly woman shuffled in, wearing a black peacoat and gray headscarf against the chill wind. She wrestled the door a bit getting it closed.

I stood to greet her, and she fixed me with a rheumy, accusatory eye. I suppressed my amusement.

"Well, you got me here. So, what do you want?"

That was interesting. Her ability was too weak for her to be certain I called her here. I sent my energy forward to read her better. She was bluffing.

"Have we met before?" My polite tone threw her off.

"Not in person."

"We've met, but not in person?"

"Something like that."

I give her a disarming smile. "Come, sit. Let's meet in person and have tea."

Loretta skirted the room, coming around the end of the gold sofa as if approaching a snake. I sat first, allowing her momentary high ground. She relaxed a bit and joined me on the golden cushion.

"Welcome to my salon."

She was busy taking in her surroundings, noting the fine art on the walls and comfortable furnishings. Her eyes lingered on the Monet above the fireplace.

"Your tea service is lovely. Don't see many vintage Victorian sets like that."

"Thank you." I poured steaming tea from the silver teapot into a finely painted porcelain cup and handed it to her. "I've had it many years."

"Ah, an heirloom, then?"

"No, I bought it new."

She shot me a dubious look over the rim of her cup. I ignored it and poured for myself, then settled back on the cushion to wait.

"Everything here is familiar."

"How so?"

Loretta's aura screamed reluctance. Accustomed to being in control, here she was unsure. She could sense the differences between us.

"Maybe I came here once, a long time ago?"

I smiled at her deflection. "I would have remembered you."

She struggled with herself for a moment, then her

shoulders dropped. "I had a dream."

"What sort of dream?"

"Just you and this salon. But the fact I dreamed at all is something. I'm old. I don't sleep good and I don't dream much. Or if I do, I stopped remembering them years ago. But this one was bright as a new penny."

"And so here you are." I sipped my tea.

"And so here I am." She fell silent.

The ticking of the grandfather clock in the corner grew in my ears, but I shut it out. Loretta sipped her tea and fussed with her handbag. I let the silence stretch.

"I don't know what I'm even doing here." Her voice was thick with annoyance.

"Am I not what you expected?"

"I don't know."

Local pressure flexed and Jeremy appeared, floating through the front window of the salon, as he liked to do.

Loretta choked on her tea. I gave her a concerned look and she waved it away, but accepted the tiny, embroidered napkin that I handed over. She patted her chin dry, white cloth bright against her sallow skin. The questions in her eyes were sharp and pointed as needles. She could not see him, but she felt his presence.

"Who are you?"

"A friend, if you wish."

"No, I mean it. Something's going on here and I want to know who, or what, you are."

"Loretta, I'm not anything you would understand, but I assure you I am not dangerous, or a threat to you in any way."

Her eyes bugged at my use of her name, and she put her teacup on the table. Though her hands were unsteady, she leaned toward me.

"I'm over ninety years old. It doesn't really matter if

135

you're a threat. I can't fight off a mosquito anymore."

I laughed at this, and she sat back in surprise. I do not laugh often, and it came out creaky and over loud. Her features were painted with confusion. I recovered myself and patted her knee.

"I truly mean you no harm, Loretta. Please, have more tea."

Jeremy hung frozen by the window, waiting for our exchange to end. As I poured more tea for my guest, he began a slow progression toward the reading room. Loretta ignored her cup and stared around the lobby, not able to see Jeremy but sure he was there. Her milky eyes made a sweep from the window to the reading room door along with his spirit. I sipped my tea and waited.

"Something is in this building."

"Yes."

"You know about it?"

"Yes."

"It comes here all the time? It haunts this building?"

"That is another interpretation, yes."

"How do you know it's a good ghost?"

"He is my friend. He will not harm you."

"He's your friend?" I did not like her mocking tone. "What's his name?"

"Jeremy."

I could see her mind working over everything, sorting facts and not liking how the math came out. She was in over her head. Grumpy indignation kicked into overdrive, and she forgot she could not even fight off a mosquito. She sat up and squared her shoulders.

"Alright look. I don't know what's going on but I'm old too for this business. So either tell me what you want, or I'm going home."

I sat my cup next to hers on the table and faced her. "It's

very simple, Loretta. I want you to come visit me."

Confusion overtook impatience. This was the last thing she expected me to say. Until the next thing I said.

"Come visit you? You mean, come over once a week and visit? I have bridge club on Thursdays, church Wednesdays and Sundays, bingo at the VFW on Mondays. I usually watch NCIS on Tuesdays. I don't have time, really."

"No, no. I want you to come visit me when you're dead."

This derailed her. She primed herself for a temper tantrum the likes of which only the infantile or the ancient can pull off. She tried to lever herself off of the sofa in indignation, but I was quicker getting to my feet.

"Sit down." I stood over her, compelling her with my body language to keep her seat. She complied, but shot me a glare and opened her mouth to protest. I cut her off.

"You are a brat."

Loretta gasped.

"You are a ninety year old brat, and you have some growing up to do. Fortunately, I can help you with that. Unfortunately, it will have to be after you die."

"How dare you say such a thing to me?"

"I would ask you the same question on the behalf of a girl named Diane, and countless others you have encountered in your lifetime."

She looked as if I slapped her. In a way, I suppose I did. Nothing was said for a long time. At last, she took a deep breath.

"I don't know what to do."

I gathered my skirt and resumed my seat on the gold sofa next to her. I reached out to pat her hand and it twitched as if she wanted to pull away, but did not.

"You will be able to find me easily, any time you want. I have never before invited a living person to visit me after death, but in your case, I have made an exception."

She snorted at me. "Am I supposed to feel honored?"

"Feel any way you wish. The invitation stands."

"Why does it have to be after I die?"

"Because after you die, certain knowledge is imparted to you that will help your understanding when you visit me. If I had encountered you years ago, I could have guided you in life. As it is, it must be this way."

"What kind of knowledge?"

"I don't know. It's different for everyone, the questions asked and answers received. But I will say this: you have been careless with your abilities these past ninety years. You have Touched the lives of others and you'll do it again in the next life because you've learned nothing in this one. Rather than see you leave a path of destruction in your wake, I choose to invite you into my home, to learn and grow."

"I feel a bit bullied, you standing over me the way you did."

"My apologies, of course."

Her lips looked like she bit a sour apple. "This is crazy. You're crazy."

"That is another interpretation, yes."

Loretta hissed like a scalded cat and snatched up her purse. This time she was quick to push herself upright, and was off the sofa and headed to the exit before I got to my feet. The bells above the door were shrill when she yanked it open. She stopped when I called her name.

"The invitation stands, Loretta."

Silence.

"I'll think about it." The grumbled words blew back in with the slamming door, her ninety-year-old arm showing surprising force.

Jeremy floated in from the reading room. "Do you think

she will show up?"

"Perhaps."

"How long?"

"She has her own time."

I avoided his question though I knew the answer, because I feared it would upset the two men. Loretta Park would die a year to the day after Jeremy's mother. He and Jeff would go Home to greet her and never return, leaving me alone in my salon with only occasional customers and visits from Mrs. Nichols to break up the time. I knew this, and accepted it. A year of solitude was nothing for me. They would not understand.

Six weeks later, Jeremy and I were settled in for a quiet evening when Jeff arrived with news. The time had come. They were going Home. The men came to me with arms open, and I reached out to them. Our hands touched, flesh and spirit, and I felt a warmth in my soul that can only be described as an embrace of hearts.

We said nothing. There were no words that needed to pass between us. They faded away, joy emanating from their souls so deep that the room thrummed with it for hours afterward. Before dawn, when the last traces of their bliss faded, I lit a bundle of sage and smudged the house, going room to room and getting every corner. No trace of them remained.

Mrs. Nichols made an appearance the following night, slinking in the front door like a stray cat and sniffing the purified air.

"The parasites are gone." Her voice was a rasp.

"They were not parasites, thank you. But yes, they are gone."

"Well, I like it a lot better around here without them." She slithered to the gold sofa. I did not respond, but poured her tea and sat down.

"Did the old crone show up yet?"

"You're full of compliments this evening, aren't you?"

"It's the new moon. I'm cranky. So, did the old bag show up yet or not?"

I frowned at her, but it made no impression. "She has not died yet."

"Oh. Well that's too bad."

"I don't know that she will accept my invitation."

"Did you tell her that you're world renowned, highly skilled, and virtually immortal?"

"Why would I tell her those things?"

Mrs. Nichols' eyes glittered at me behind her spectacles. "Well, they're true, aren't they?"

"Perhaps, But not necessary details for her at this stage."

"You just don't like tooting your own horn."

"That's another interpretation, yes."

"I've been watching Diane. She's doing better."

I shot her a look. "Do not interfere with Diane, Mrs. Nichols."

She held up her gnarled, knobby hands to ward me off. "Don't worry, don't worry. I was just watching."

"Again, do not interfere."

Mrs. Nichols snorted at me. "She's boring, anyhow."

"You leave Loretta Park alone, too."

She cut her eyes at me, perturbed that I anticipated her thought process. No response was made, which I took as a good sign she would heed my wishes. Loretta Park needed to come to me if and when she was ready, no other way.

Mrs. Nichols drained three cups of tea then took her leave, melting away into the winter darkness as if she were made of shadows herself. Over the next several months, she returned more often and stayed longer with each visit. The absence of my objectionable spirit friends made her more comfortable in my home, and she took advantage.

The following year passed as many do, uneventful and forgettable. In spring I stayed busy, thanks to bumper crops of houndsbane and liverwort. Summer brought strawberry wine and long nights at the telescope plotting movements of constellations. I missed Jeremy and Jeff, but for the most part I was content with my own company.

At last the day came, however. I sat in my reading room in my wingback chair, book open on my lap and a pot of tea on the table. Loretta Park's spirit floated through the wall and directly up to me. I smiled in welcome.

"I've been to the Q&A Room. You were right. I'm a brat."

8. SPEARFINGER
By MARK COOK

Thursday, 6:10 A.M.

The phone vibrated on the nightstand. Another baby is dead.

Eric Weller rolled to his left and tried to find the phone in the dark. Twice his hand bumped it, but he couldn't get a handle on it. The third time he knocked it off the nightstand onto the linoleum below. The phone stopped just as he picked it up.

The octopus sheet entangled his legs as Eric tried to get up. As he stood and stretched out his five-foot, four-inch frame, the phone began to ring again. "Weller," he said his voice rough from too many cigarettes and Crown from the night before.

"Hi, handsome. Time to go to work. They found another one." It was Ginger, the night dispatcher. Her bubbly voice made Eric want to climb through the phone and pull her tongue out of her mouth.

"Where?"

"About a mile north of Blue Hole off Kenwood Road," the voice smiled through the phone.

Weller sighed, "I'm on my way. Tell them not to touch anything 'til I get there." He hung up the phone and made his way to the bathroom. The picture in the mirror was disgusting. Too much booze, lack of sleep, and long hours at work were showing. It felt like he had new wrinkles every time he looked into the glass soul catcher. He threw cold water on his face, spread it around his neck, and wiped his bloodshot eyes. It was going to be another long day.

It was about a 25-minute drive from Eric's house west of Pryor to where they found the body. His 1974 Ford Pinto growled and whined the whole way there. He pulled over off the road onto the flint-rock bank of Saline Creek. Two Mayes County patrol units, a Cherokee Nation Marshal's unit, and a state coroner's van were already there. Crime scene tape and a cluster of uniformed officers told him where the body was. The forensic team was nowhere to be found.

Weller ducked under the crime scene tape and joined the crowd. "Who was first on the scene?" he growled.

"That would be me," Deputy Morris said as he walked over, his head down with his hands in his pockets.

"Why are all these people in my crime scene? Get everyone back. How the hell are we supposed to find evidence with all these people trampling all over it?" Eric didn't try to hide his disgust. "Get them out!"

"Yes, sir." Morris shuffled everyone outside the tape, embarrassed that he broke the first rule of securing the crime scene.

"Where is the forensic team?"

"Still ten minutes out. They were working a burglary in Chouteau."

"Have these other numb nuts that are standing around with their teeth in their mouth to start working the perimeter, a quarter mile up and down the creek. Bag everything they see. Send two people across the creek to do the same."

"Yes, sir." Morris nearly fell over his own feet running over to the law officers and getting them started to work.

Weller walked over to where the body lay half submerged in the creek. Her blue dress danced in the water as the current pushed against her body. Small debris brought by the current outlined the up-river side of her body.

Weller put on a pair of plastic gloves and stepped around the body, wishing he had worn his water-resistant boots. Cold water gushed into his leather boots, probably ruining them. Weller searched around the body. There was evidence of fish eating on the body, but from what he could see, no varmints had touched her.

Brakes squealed from the road, and a Ford Transit Cargo van with Mayes County Forensics on the side rolled down from the highway narrowly missing the Cherokee Nation Marshal's SUV, and rested against a small tree just in front of the crime scene. A skinny man with glasses and a quart of grease in his hair climbed out of the van and immediately went around the back and popped the rear doors open. When he came back around the front, he was carrying two large plastic cases. Stumbling over undergrowth and slipping on loose rocks, he finally made it to where Weller stood.

"Howdy Weller."

"Minks. Glad you could make it." Weller said through his gritted teeth.

"Sorry, it took so long. Must be a full moon or something." Minks set his cases on the bank, slipped on gloves, and pulled a laser tape measure and a pad of paper out of one of the cases. "I haven't been home since I started my shift yesterday morning." Minks measured the distance of the body from the shore. "Had a knife fight at the strip joint on 412, a lady damn near cut her boyfriend's jewels off, and then a burglary at the Dollar General."

Weller walked to the bank and looked up and down the creek. "Morris!"

"Yyyyes sir," Morris said as he ran to Weller.

"Ginger said some guys fishing found the body. Where are they?"

"I took their statements and let them go. No use ruining the rest of their day."

"You let them go. This is a murder investigation and you just let our only potential witnesses go?

"Yes sir. I got their names though. They're camping up the creek a ways."

"Give me their names and take me to where they're camping. Minks, let me know what you find. Tell the coroner this is top priority."

"Will do."

Deputy Morris had problems hiking the quarter mile to the campsite. His six-foot frame carried an extra 70 pounds of fried food and donuts. Add to that he dipped a can of Skoal Long Cut Wintergreen every shift. Although he was only twenty-seven, he looked like he was about to have a heart attack before they even got half way.

"Just point me in the right direction Morris. I don't have all day"

Morris, his hands on both knees pointed through the trees on the other side of the creek. Weller took off at a pace most fit teenagers would have a problem keeping up with.   He crossed the creek, fought through the underbrush, and came out into a little clearing. The fishermen were gone. They broke camp and were probably halfway home by now.

Weller poked around until he found where they had parked their vehicle about two hundred yards from the clearing. "Crap. What a waste." There wasn't much else he could do but go back to the crime scene. When he got back, there were two Oklahoma State Bureau of Investigation SUVs and a Channel 6 News van parked along the road. Three men in khakis and Polos were standing inside his crime scene. One had his back turned and was on his cell phone, the other two stood talking with Minks.

"Weller, look who we have visiting. Three honest to goodness OSBI agents all the way from Tahlequah." Minks smiled as if he knew what was about to happen.

"Get out of my crime scene," Weller barked at the men.

"Whoa there Ant Man. we're here to..." He never finished his sentence. One second he was standing like he owned the place; the next he was rolling down the bank into Saline Creek. When he stood, his clothes were leaking creek water out the sleeves and pant legs. The second OSBI agent started forward. The look on Weller's face stopped him cold.

The third agent ended his call and turned around to find out what the commotion was. "What's going on here. Billings what are you doing in the river?"

Minks laughed and said, "It's a creek Mr. OSBI agent. Saline Creek to be exact." OSBI agents were used to running roughshod over local departments.

"I'm agent Dan Holcomb. I repeat. What's going on here?"

Weller walked over to him and stood close. "Your agents

are in my crime scene. Get them out or I will. Your choice."

Holcomb looked Weller over from head to toe. Short, well built, long sandy red hair in a ponytail, work boots, blue jeans, and a t-shirt that said "1776 percent pure American". When he got to his eyes he stopped. Dead green eyes stared back at him. Holcomb had seen friendlier eyes in a rattlesnake. "Billings, Renfro, get out of this man's crime scene." He turned back to Weller. "I didn't get your name."

"I didn't give it."

"Alright for now. I'm sure we'll meet up again. Say, who do you work for?"

"The people of Mayes County."

Holcomb and his team walked toward their SUVs. When Billings walked by Weller, he said in a low voice, "We're not done here."

"We better be for your sake."

Weller walked over to Minks. "I want everything you find ASAP. Leave nothing out. If we don't find a clue pretty quick, more kids are going to die." Weller turned and walked up the hill to find Morris. "I want this place sealed off until you hear from me. Nobody gets near it without my say so. Understand?"

"Yes, sir. I'll stay here myself." Morris said as if he were a puppy trying to make his master happy.

"I can't tell you what a relief that is," Weller said not caring if Morris caught his sarcasm. Weller crawled into the Pinto and drove off.

Morris walked over to the crime scene and stood like a Palace Guard protecting the crown jewels. Billings and Renfro walked down the hill to speak with Morris.

"Who the hell was that?" Billings said pointing his head towards the fleeing Pinto.

"That's Weller. He's the Mayes County investigator," Morris said shifting from foot to foot. He probably should not be talking to them, but they were the OSBI.

"Does he have a little man's syndrome or what?" Renfro asked.

"Don't guess so. Never really thought about it. I don't think Weller knows he's little." Before he could stop of himself, he said, "Sure didn't seem to have a problem taking him down."

Billings' face turned crimson. He started to say something but instead walked back up to where Holcomb stood.

"So, what's Weller's story?" Renfro said trying to buddy up to Morris.

"I don't think anyone knows for sure, leastways the other deputies. I snuck into the personnel files once to try to find out. His file wasn't there. Come to find out its locked in the Sheriff's file cabinet." Morris stopped talking long enough to put a healthy dip of Skoal Long Cut Wintergreen in his lip. "I can tell you not to mess with him. Those that do usually end up in the hospital.

"Tough guy, is he?"

"By looking at him, you wouldn't think so. I've seen him in action though." Morris stopped talking long enough to spit some tobacco juice on a black ant wandering by. "Uh few months ago, I got called out to back him up at a biker bar on Highway 20. I got there just in time to see Weller square off against a badass biker named Smitty."

"Took him out huh?"

"To be honest with you. I don't know what happened. I know one-minute Smitty was swearing at Weller and the next second he was laying on the ground choking to death. Nobody saw what happened and we were all standing right there. Weller looked at Smitty's friends and told them, "I don't like profanity around women. You boys best be getting Smitty to the hospital 'for he dies. He's got about twenty minutes if he's lucky. Tell him when he gets out to turn himself in at the county courthouse, or I'll come looking for him."

"Did he?"

"Damn straight he did. Two days later he came strolling into the county jail and turned himself in. Been there ever since."

"Interesting. Nice talking with you, deputy. I'm sure I'll be seeing you around. Tell Weller to walk lightly around Billings. Billings holds a grudge."

Morris laughed. "I'm sure Weller won't sleep a wink knowing he hurt that poor man's feelings."

Thursday, 10:30 P.M.

Weller was furious. Not at the OSBI, but at himself. He shouldn't let idiots get to him. With nothing to investigate until he got Mink's and the coroner's reports, Weller stopped by The East Side Diner for breakfast. He sat at the far end of restaurant with his back to the wall, away from the plate glass windows that covered the front. The waitresses all knew him and brought him his usual of hot black coffee, orange juice, two eggs over easy, bacon, and two slices of wheat toast. No one else in town could match their food or the excellent service. His phone rang just as he was finishing his toast.

"Weller," he answered washing his last bite down with coffee.

"You've been a really bad boy haven't you?" It was Ginger's day shift equivalent, Aileen.

"What do you want Aileen?" He said trying not to scream at the annoying voice coming over the phone.

"Well sugar, it sounds like you got up on the wrong side of the bed this morning. Maybe you could come by my house after work and let Aileen take care of you. Maybe relieve some of that stress."

"Sorry, Aileen I'm busy. Did you call me for a reason or did you just want to sexually harass me?"

Aileen giggled into the phone. "Sheriff wants to see you an hour ago. Rumor has it some OSBI guy came in raising Cain about you. Some guy named Holcomb."

"Wonderful. I'll be in soon."

"Better sooner than later honey, unless we're talking about something else. You know what I mean?"

Weller hung up as an answer. He left a five-dollar tip on the table and paid his check near the front door. Racehorse pictures on the wall behind the register reminded Weller of his rodeo days in high school. Happier times.

Thursday, 1:00 P.M.

Weller parked by the jail and walked around to the sheriff's office. The few people that saw him waved or greeted him with the nod of their heads. Sheriff Bill Thomas sat at his desk going over paperwork. Thomas wasn't a huge man, standing six foot even with 200 pounds insulating his bones and muscles. Lately, due to the overwhelming paperwork and riding a desk, he was starting to insulate his stomach area more than normal. His black hair was starting to gray on the sides, and his once thick black mustache was now nearly all gray.

Weller tapped on the window embedded into the large oak door to the sheriff's office. Thomas glanced up from his paperwork and motioned Weller in. Weller entered the office and stood by a leather chair on the other side of Thomas' desk. "Sit." The sheriff rubbed his eyes and leaned back in his chair. Doing as ordered, Weller pulled the chair back and plopped down into it. "Tell me about this morning."

Weller told him every detail about the latest body and the crime scene. When he finished, Thomas sat quiet for a moment and then leaned forward in his chair, placing his elbows on the overcrowded desk. "Tell me about knocking the OSBI agent into the creek."

"You heard about that huh?" Sheriff Thomas nodded his head. "It was stupid. I lost my cool. I was still mad about the crime scene being compromised, and then I came back and saw people I didn't know in my crime scene. I sorta lost it."

"I heard one of the agents made a disparaging remark about you. That true."

"I guess you have been talking to Minks. It's true, but it was more about those suits in my crime scene."

Thomas was lost in a moment of thought. For several moments, not a word was spoken, and then he burst out in uncontrollable laughter. A secretary walked by concerned that maybe the sheriff had finally lost it. Weller shifted in his seat not knowing how to take the sheriff's behavior.

"I'm sorry. But Ant Man, seriously. He deserved to be knocked on his butt. I wish I have been there. Don't worry about those guys. I'll take care of them. But I have some bad news. A task force was formed, and you're part of it. The OSBI is in charge."

"Now wait a minute! I can't work for those imbeciles. They couldn't find their butts if they had a hole in their pants!"

"Hear me out. I know you don't want to work with them. I understand, and I don't blame you. I need someone on the task force to represent Mayes County. I can't, and you're the best we have. Just give it a shot. If it doesn't work out, I'll get Morris to be on it.

"Morris, seriously. He's a really nice guy, but he has no experience investigating murders."

"That's why I need you. Will you give it a shot please?"

"Alright," Weller said after a moment of soul-searching. "I can't promise you how it will turn out though."

"Fair enough. You have a task force meeting in the courthouse conference room in ten minutes."

Thursday, 1:30 P.M.

Weller walked into the conference room at precisely 1:30. The conference room had a long table with black vinyl chairs lining both sides. Four telephones were in the middle of the table along with glasses and pitchers of water. Notepads and pens were in front of each chair. Coffee was available from a stainless-steel decanter along the far wall. Stacks of Styrofoam cups stood guard to the right of the dispenser. On the front wall, was a large television and a portable whiteboard. The three murder victim's pictures hung along the top of the whiteboard. The two missing children's pictures ended the row.

Weller sat down in a chair closest to the door. Next to him sat George Longfeather from the Cherokee County Sheriff's office, Mike Walkingbear from the Cherokee Nation Marshal's office, John Tyler from the Rogers County Sheriff's office, and a computer geek from down in the basement. Across from Weller sat Renfro, Billings, and the young lady from the crime scene. At the head of the table, was Holcomb, of course.

Holcomb stood up and went to the whiteboard. "This task force has been formed to find the killer or killers of these girls. This is an election year, and the governor isn't happy. Serial killers are bad for business. Before we get started, I'd like everyone to introduce themselves and tell what department you're with. Weller ignored everyone until it got to the young lady sitting across from the table.

"My name is Laura Swift. I'm a psychologist. I work as a consultant for the OSBI."

Great, three idiots and a shrink, Weller thought as he stared at the pretty young psychologist.

"Alright, now we know who we are all working with. Ms. Swift, can you tell us what you've come up with so far?"

"Thank you, Agent Holcomb. I've done a preliminary profile from the information I have received. I think we are looking for a white male, age 24-35 who has issues with women...

"Jesus," Weller said what he thought was under his breath.

"Excuse me?" Swift's blue eyes shot out flames toward Weller. Billings smiled across the table at him.

"Lady, nothing personal, but you have no idea what you're talking about. We don't have any clues to lead us to anyone. The girls just disappear, and then show up dead. There are no links to the victims other than they are about the same age and all three are Native Americans. We have no leads and as of right now, nothing to go on."

"This is just a preliminary hypothesis I've worked up by your own reports. Do you have any other information you can share that will help us?" She demanded.

"No, ma'am. I don't want these men to go back to their offices and tell their officers to look for something or someone that doesn't exist. It's a waste of manpower."

"Mr. Weller," Holcomb butted in. "Surely you can see how Ms. Swift's report can be of use to you out in the field."

"Not really. I'll listen to Ms. Swift when she has enough information for a suspect profile. But not now." He got up and walked out of the room.

Weller walked straight to his waiting steed and drove off. Instead of going home, he drove out to Hooker's Sports Bar and Grill on the south end of Pryor. Weller took out his Glock 19 still holstered in his Alien Gear paddle holster and put it in the glove box. As he got out of his car, a red Mustang pulled in. Swift got out of the Mustang.

"You buying?"

Weller was too stunned to answer, so he turned and walked into the bar. He could hear the clatter of high heels as Swift tried to catch up.

In the middle of the afternoon, Hooker's was nearly empty. The staff rushed around filling up ketchup bottles and salt and pepper shakers. The bartender was bringing cases of beer from the back and filling the coolers under the bar.

Weller took his usual spot in the far corner, backed up to the wall. Swift sat down opposite him and stared at him.

"You know you didn't have to disrespect me in front of everyone!" Darts flew from Swift's eyes.

Weller looked down at his hands tilting the shakers. Then he raised his eyes onto to Swift's. "I'm sorry. No disrespect was intended. Sometimes I lose my cool. This case is just so frustrating. We have three dead little girls and no clues. No forensics, no witnesses, nothing. We are just waiting around for another little girl to die."

After a moment, Swift's eyes softened, and she began seeing Weller in another way. "Apology accepted as long as it doesn't happen again." Swift took out a spiral notebook like the reporters used and a pen from her purse. "Can I ask you a question?"

"Ask away."

"You said I didn't have all the information about these cases. I read every report that was turned in."

"We don't put everything in the reports. Reports can be leaked. Investigations can be ruined." The waitress came over and smiled at Weller.

"Hi, Eric. Long time no see."

"Hey, Lynn. How have you been?" Swift could see Weller was getting more uncomfortable by the second. He started playing with the salt shaker, tilting it one way and then the next.

"Just peachy. By the way, thanks for the wham bam thank you, ma'am."

By now Weller was shifting uncomfortably in the vinyl booth. "You're welcome. You think I could get a Bud Light and something for the lady?"

Lynn was enjoying torturing him. "Why sure dreamboat. What'll you have ma'am?"

Swift was enjoying the show. "I'll have a rum and Coke please, easy on the Coke." Swift never took her eyes off Weller who seemed to be getting smaller the longer Lynn stuck around.

"Coming right up." To the relief of Weller, Lynn walked away to get their orders.

"Wow, that was kind of awkward," Swift grinned.

"How do you mean? Just another crazy woman with marriage on her mind." Weller grinned back. There was something about Swift that interested him. Of course, she was beautiful. Her long brunette hair reached half-way down her back, and her deep blue eyes looked like the polished surface of a calm lake when she smiled. She had a figure that no business suit could hide. But that was the physical part. There was something else attracting him to her.

"I guess in small towns you can never get away from your conquests, huh?"

"It was a one-night fling. Too much alcohol and not

enough sense. Let's change the subject." Weller set the salt shaker back down on the wooden table and slid it back in to place next to the pepper.

Swift decided to let him off the hook. "You said not everything is in the reports. What was left out, and why?"

"Reporters seem to know as much as we do. I don't put gut feelings, theories, etc. in reports. I've been burned too many times to take a chance."

"Okay, what was left out of your reports for this investigation?"

Weller thought a moment before answering. Swift noticed the hesitation. 'You can trust me. We're on the same side, remember."

"You're OSBI. The last big case the OSBI was invited in by the sheriff, one of the agents ran his mouth off in a restaurant. Someone overheard him." Weller picked back up the salt shaker and started tilting it back and forth. "Because of that agent running his mouth, the news stations got a hold of the story, and an innocent man died because of it. It wasn't Billings, but someone just as ignorant."

"I'm sorry." Swift took the salt shaker from Weller's hand and put it down. "I'm a consultant, not an agent. I need to know everything if I'm going to help stop whoever is killing these little girls."

When Weller hesitated, Swift leaned in. "Do you remember the girls who were murdered at the Girl Scout camp near Locust Grove in the late s'70s?" Weller nodded his head and Swift continued. "My aunt was one of those girls. It was my mom's older sister. I never got to meet her because some psycho decided to murder her and two other innocent little girls. They never caught the real killer. I want to help catch this killer. I want their families to have some sort of closure. My mom and my grandparents never got that closure."

The whole time she was talking, Weller was watching her closely. Her eyes never wavered from his. After years of interrogating Afghan villagers looking for the Taliban, he could tell who was telling the truth. Swift was. With no leads in the investigation, Weller decided to trust Swift.

"The victims' livers were cut out. The coroner says it was a six to eight- inch blade that was very rough. It was almost like the livers had been sawed out." George Strait singing Amarillo by Morning interrupted. It was coming from Weller's phone. He looked at the display and then answered, "What have you got Minks?"

"You need to come to the lab as soon as you can." Minks whispered. "Come in the back way, though. That OSBI agent Holcomb is looking for your scalp. Don't go anywhere near the sheriff's office or the main lobby."

"I'll be there in ten." Turning to Swift, he said, "Drinks will have to wait. Minks has something." Weller stood, placed a ten-dollar bill on the table for the drinks they never got and walked toward the door. Halfway there, he turned to the still seated Swift. "You comin'?"

Thursday, 3:30 P.M.

"Whatta you got Minks?" Weller said as he swept into the lab followed by Swift in her high heels.

"I'm not sure. But it may be something." Minks rolled in his chair from his desk over to a microscope. "Take a look."

"What am I looking for?" Minks just pointed. Weller looked into the microscope. He saw what looked like a black thorn, or bone. It was two or three inches long with a pointed tip on one end and came to a flat edge on the other. "What is it?" he said as Swift moved him out of the way with her shoulder and looked for herself.

"I'm not sure," Minks said rolling back over to his desk. "At first I thought it was a stick lodged in Grace's hair."

"Who's?"

"Grace. Grace Greencorn. The little girl in Saline Creek."

So that was her name. Weller tried not to focus on names. It was his way of not making it personal. It never worked, but he still tried.

Swift picked up the evidence and looked it over. "Its smooth," she said turning it over and over in her hand. "It's not like any thorn I've ever seen though. It's very light."

"Have you showed this to Holcomb?"

"No. As far as I'm concerned, this is your case. The OSBI can suck a big one." Minks put his feet up on his desk and leaned back in his chair. "Of course, I'll have to share eventually, but I should be able to keep it under wraps for a day or two."

"You do that. Bag that up. I'm taking it with me."

"You got it." Minks said walking over to the microscope. He pulled an evidence bag from the shelf, marked it, and handed it to Swift. "Technically we are not withholding evidence from the OSBI now." Minks had just put Swift smack dab in the middle of a jurisdiction battle. Judging by the look on Swift's face, it was clear to her, too.

"Hey, you guys heard about the missing girl?"

"What girl?"

"I didn't catch the name, but she's been missing a few days. They found her shoes in the West Side Tavern parking lot. Phil had the car towed, so we picked it up to check for evidence. Getting ready to go through it now."

"Good luck. Let's go, Swift," Weller said heading toward the door at a fast pace. "Before Holcomb gets wind that we're down here."

Part Two

Friday, 9 A.M.

Weller woke to a pounding on the door. "Jesus, calm down. I'm coming." Weller stumbled to the front door wearing only his Scooby-Doo boxers and a frown. He flung the door open to find Swift standing there like a goddess. She wore tight Wranglers that formed perfectly to her long legs. A blue business-like top even looked sexy on Swift.

"You finished drooling? I've been knocking on the door for ten minutes." Swift moved past Weller and into the tiny living room. "Get your pants on Shaggy. Holcomb is on his way. He found out about the evidence."

"Crap. Okay. Hold your horses," Weller said grabbing his jeans off the floor and stepping through the legs. "How did he find out so quick?"

"Not sure. Minks has been trying to call you for more than an hour. He finally called my hotel room." Swift walked over to the closet, swept clothes along the rod out of the way, and chose a blue Polo. "Here," she said tossing the shirt to Weller as he finished putting his boots on. "Come on. My car is parked out back. We'll come back and get your stallion later." Without waiting for a reply, she walked out the back door. Weller followed throwing on the shirt and grabbing his holstered Glock 19 off the nightstand.

Instead of using Highway 20 back into town, Weller showed Swift how to take the backroads to Adair and then south down Highway 69 to Pryor. "Turn left at the light just past the smoke shop. Then take a left at the last light past downtown."

"Where we going?" Swift said taking a left at the last light after downtown.

"Breakfast. Then we'll go talk to Grace's parents."

Swift pulled in to the parking lot of the East Side Diner and parked near the front door. At this time of morning, most people were already working. The only people in the diner were older folks who didn't have to be anywhere at any particular time. Weller envied them and hoped to make it to that point in his life. With his job and lifestyle, it wasn't likely.

Weller led Swift to his usual table. After they ordered coffee and breakfast they had a chance to talk.

"I ran you in the FBI databases."

"And…"

"Let's see. Army Green Beret, two tours of Afghanistan, two Silver Stars, nominated for the Medal of Honor, four purple hearts, an honorable discharge about five years ago after ten years of military service. That's a pretty interesting career. I also noticed the bullet scar on your chest and the scars on your back this morning."

"Scars are life's little road map."

"After the military, there's not much other than an assault charge in Memphis about four years ago that was dropped. No big surprise there with your temper.

Weller smiled and asked, "So now that you know my background, what does that tell you about me?"

"You want me to profile you?"

"You already have. So, tell me about me."

"Well, let's see. Judging by your background report and what I've seen, I'd say you are a ladies' man who has commitment issues. You don't like authority, but you like structure. You have a temper that can go from cool to boiling in a split second, and you like making a difference in people's lives. How's that?"

Weller tilted the salt shaker back and forth. "Hit and miss. I can hold my temper in check when I want to. I don't like stupid and I don't like bullies. That arrest in Memphis was bogus. A guy was slapping his wife around in front of my apartment. I took exception."

"Two broken ribs, a broken nose, and three teeth knocked out is quite the exception."

"He should have quit while he could. Now it's my turn."

Swift raised her eyebrows but kept her eyes focused on Weller. "Okay, go for it."

"I ran a report on you last night, too. I needed to know if I could trust you. You're thirty-one years old. Born in Tahlequah. Your mom is a Cherokee citizen, but you're not. You worked your way through school and earned a master' degree from the University of Oklahoma. You're beautiful, but you don't use that to your advantage. And you believe in justice. How's that?"

Swift smiled, but breakfast arrived and delayed her response. "Not bad for an Ant Man." After leaving a tip and paying, they pulled out of the parking lot and drove toward Kenwood.

Grace Greencorn's family lived just east of Kenwood. As they drove through the community, Weller noticed an old man sitting on a bench outside the convenience store as they drove by. "Turn left at the next road. According to my map, they live about a half mile down that road on a small tick and chigger farm."

"Why don't you use the GPS on your phone?"

"These houses aren't usually on the map. The GPS will get you lost more times than not."

"Do they really raise ticks and chiggers?" Swift asked trying to figure out if Weller was kidding or not.

"Might as well. Those are the only things that grow here. And flint rocks. Can't forget those. I guess I left gullible out your profile."

The road ended at a small mobile home sitting on cement blocks. Chickens roamed around in the front yard. On the porch, a lazy dog lifted his head at them and then went back to sleep. A skinny horse was penned up in a small wire corral off to the left. A refrigerator and an old tractor collected rust on the right.

A man appeared on the front porch. Behind him, three children stuck their heads out the door to see who was there.

The man met them before they got out of their car. "What do you want?" he said with no emotion in his voice.

"Mr. Greencorn, I'm Eric Weller from the sheriff's office. This is Ms. Swift. We came to talk to you about your daughter."

"I'm talked out. Some other investigators were here last night. We don't know anything. One minute we were swimming at Blue Hole with Grace, the next minute she was gone. We thought the creek might have got her, but she's a good swimmer. Or was." The whole time Greencorn was talking the other children were getting closer and closer to the car.

"Can we talk to your other children? Maybe they saw or heard something."

"You can. But them kids would've told me if they'd seen anything."

"Is Mrs. Greencorn home?"

"She is, but the doc over at the hospital in Claremore gave her something to help her calm down. She has been mostly sleeping the last few days. Took several pills yesterday when they told us about Grace." Mr. Greencorn seemed to be holding on by a thread.

"We won't disturb her then. We'll talk to the kids and be on our way." Greencorn shrugged and walked back inside his castle.

Swift interviewed the children while Weller sat on the porch and petted the dog. When she finished with the last child, they headed back down the dirt road. A cloud of dust chased them to the pavement where Swift stopped and put the car in neutral.

"Did you get anything out of the children?" Weller asked.

"Not much," Swift hesitated. "Maybe."

"What?"

"One of the other daughters said she saw Grace talking to an old lady."

"Maybe it's something. Did you get a description?"

"Not much. She said she was very old and stooped over. She said she wore old clothes like the people at the cultural center wear."

Weller sat in thought for a moment. "Get out. I'm driving." Weller got out and walked around the Mustang. Swift sat where she was. "Come on get out."

"Why?"

"Where we're going it is a sign of weakness for the woman to be driving," Weller lied. He just wanted to drive the muscle car.

Swift got out, but she wasn't happy. She stomped around the Mustang, got in and slammed the door hard enough to knock a maggot off a horse dumpling.

Weller ignored her anger and put the car in gear with his right hand and scratched his head with his left.

A mile down the road Swift asked, "Did you get anything from the dog?"

"Fleas." They rode in silence until they arrived at the Kenwood convenience store.

"Why are we stopping here?"

"I want to talk to some of the people around here. Maybe they know who this old lady is. This store is kind of like the meeting place in this community. Sit tight."

"Why can't I go in?"

"You'll distract them. I want their full attention. Besides you look like you might work for the Feds. They don't much care for the government."

"Why?"

Weller rolled the windows down and got out. "You ever hear of The Trail of Tears?" The old man was still sitting on the bench. When Weller walked by, he said something very softly in Cherokee. Weller stopped. "Excuse me?" Once again, the old man mumbled in Cherokee. Weller walked on in the store and asked about Grandma. Nobody recognized the description, or at least nobody would admit to it. Local lawmen weren't tolerated much more than Feds. Weller grabbed a couple of Dr. Peppers and went to pay at the counter. A teenaged boy was working the counter. "Do you know what Yunwi Tsunsdi means?"

"'Fraid not. I don't speak Cherokee. You might try the man out by the gas pumps." Weller looked out the glass doors and saw an old Ford F-150 with an even older horse trailer hooked to the rear. A middle-aged man was feeding the Ford.

"Thanks." Weller took the Dr. Peppers to the SUV and then walked out to the gas pumps. "Excuse me..." The man looked over from the gas pump. He looked Weller up and down and then smiled. "You must be Usdi Tsitaga Aniyvwi. What can I do for you?"

Weller wasn't sure what to say. "My name's Weller. The boy inside at the register said you might be to help me. Can you tell me what Yunwi Tsunsdi means?"

The man's smile went away instantly. He turned off the pump and slammed the handle back in its holster. As he put his gas cap back on he asked, "Where did you hear that?"

"When I walked by the old man on the bench, he mumbled it."

"Do yourself a favor. Don't say those words out loud again."

Weller was puzzled. Why would those two words make this man so angry? "What do they mean?"

The man looked at him and then got a piece of paper out of his F-250 and a pen. He scribbled on the paper, almost shoved it at Weller, and then got back in his truck and sped out of the parking lot, his tires trying to grip the gravel as he floored the accelerator.

Weller looked at the paper. All it said was:

LITTLE PEOPLE

Weller walked back to the SUV and got in. The old man looked at him and smiled. Weller was now even more confused than when the old man originally said it.

"What's wrong?" Swift asked noticing the angry and confused face of Weller.

"Nothing. Buckle up." Weller left the convenience store burning rubber as he went.

Friday, 9:00 P.M.

Weller sat alone in his living room. His laptop set on the coffee table in front of the couch. Weller Googled: Cherokee Little People. The results confused him.

There are three kinds of little people: One is the Laurel People. They are mischievous and love to spread laughter. Another is the Rock People. Rock People are evil and bring harm to children. Finally, there's the Dogwood People, who are kind and take care of people.

Why would the old Indian say that to him? A knock at

the door interrupted his thoughts. "Come in."

The door opened, and Swift walked in carrying a pizza and a six pack of Bud Light longnecks. "Boy you're a sight for sore eyes," Weller said.

"Why, thank you."

"I was talking to the Bud Light. But since you're here, have a sit. I need your brain power."

Swift walked into the kitchen and found some paper plates and napkins. She put the four beers in the fridge and brought everything else into the living room.

"What has your little brain in a frenzy?" Swift said as she bit into a slice of Stampede pizza from Pizza Corral.

"In Kenwood the other day, that old man on the bench said Yunwi Tsunsdi to me. When I asked the man at the gas pumps what it meant, he said I should never say those words aloud. Read what I found out about the Little People on Google."

Swift read while she finished off her slice of pizza and washed it down with a Bud Light.

"At first I thought he was calling me a Little People and I got pissed when I read about it. But now I'm not so sure," Weller grabbed a large slice of pizza and woofed it down.

"Maybe he was trying to tell you something."

"But what? I've been going over and over the evidence."

"Maybe they are the ones killing the girls."

"Funny, but I haven't seen any Little People around here. Have you?"

Swift typed some words on the laptop and waited for the slow Internet to give her an answer. She scanned several websites between slices of pizza and Bud Light. "It says here that Cherokees believe if you say those words out loud, they will come. It could be very dangerous.

"Bull. How could saying a few words be dangerous? It's

just superstition. Changing the subject, have you seen or talked to Holcomb?"

"I saw him earlier. He is not happy with you or me. I told him I was trying to get an accurate profile by running around with you and visiting with the locals. I have a bad feeling he is not going to write a good report about me.

"You could always work freelance. There are a lot of departments and agencies in this region of the country that could use your help. It would be better than calling the OSBI."

"It doesn't matter. What matters is finding our killer. It's getting late. I need to get going."

"Or, you could stay here," Weller said staring into her eyes.

"I think not Romeo. We have a killer to catch. Then we'll talk." Swift grabbed her purse and went through the door before Weller had a chance to reply.

Saturday, 2:30 A.M.

After Swift left, Weller cleaned up and went straight to bed. After a few hours of fitful sleep, he got up to use the bathroom. When he came back into the bedroom, he felt a presence. There was nothing he could see but after years of combat he knew to trust his instincts. He edged over to the nightstand to get his pistol. It wasn't there. He turned just in time as a spear meant for his chest sunk into his left shoulder. He staggered into the living room and fell striking his head on the coffee table. He closed his eyes briefly and popped them back open when he felt the spear being removed. Blood poured out of his wound. Through pain filled eyes he looked up and saw something so hideous, he blinked his eyes to make sure it was really there.

An old woman, hunched over like she was carrying

something very heavy on her back, look down at him with eyes that glowed yellow and seemed to reach into his soul. A mop of mostly gray hair sat on her head and ran down to her shoulders. Pointed teeth seemed to crawl out of her mouth. Fingernails six inches long, sprouted from her fingers.

She bent down close to Weller's face. Her breath smelled of old death and decay. His almost scream was cut off by a blow to his stomach that knocked his breath and maybe, his soul right out of his body. He passed out.

When Weller regained consciousness, the house was empty. Blood soaked the rug he was laying on and his new George Strait shirt. His head felt like an IED had exploded and bounced around the inside of his skull. His shoulder bled profusely. Using his uninjured arm and the arm of the couch, he pushed himself up to a standing position. Through the rockets' red glare, and bombs bursting in mid-air in his head, he found his phone and his gun on the coffee table. He slipped the Glock into its holster and put it on his hip.

Weller dialed 911 and then went out on the porch and collapsed into a camping chair to wait for them. Ten minutes later he was on his way to the Claremore Hospital. Somewhere along the way, he passed out again.

Saturday, 5:30 P.M.

Weller heard a rustling sound and reached for his gun, but it wasn't there.

"You looking for this?" Swift asked holding up the Glock.

Weller eyes slowly came into focus. What was Swift doing with his gun? He raised his head to look around the room. Instantly his head exploded, and lasers bounced around the inside of his head.

"Stay down. The doc says that on top of your shoulder nearly being torn off, you have a concussion. Lay back, and I'll raise the bed. Swift bent over Weller to find the bed controls.

"You smell like lavender. Yum."

"Easy Romeo. It's just my new perfume. It's called Suave. It cleans hair, too." Swift found the control and raised the bed so Weller could see. Holcomb and the sheriff were also in the room.

Sheriff Thomas stood up and walked over next to the bed on the other side.

He didn't look well. Saddlebags hung underneath his red eyes and he hadn't shaved. "You gave us a scare Usdi Tsitaga Aniyvwi. Doc said they had to put four pints of blood in you. Deputy Morris even gave you some of his. They were going to Lifeflight you to Tulsa, but they were afraid you wouldn't make it."

"What day is it?"

"Still Saturday," Holcomb answered walking over to the bed. "Do you remember anything about what happened?"

"Not much. I got hit with a spear. And then it is kind of blurry. I think I called 911."

"A spear. Are you sure?"

"Kind of hard to forget. It 'bout took my shoulder off."

"Did you get a look at who stabbed you?" Thomas asked.

"No. Everything is still hazy."

"Probably all the drugs you're on. You rest now. We'll come back tomorrow and talk again." Thomas ushered Holcomb out the door.

Swift grabbed Weller's hand and squeezed. He hung on for dear life. She let him. "I went to your place while you were in recovery. Morris went back out there after he gave blood. Your place was taped off, but I begged, and he relented. Don't give him a hard time about it. He was scared to death you were going to die. I thought he was going to cry when I told him you made it out of surgery and you were going to live."

Weller grimaced as Swift sat down on the edge of the bed. "Weller I need you to focus. Can you do that?" Weller nodded as he tried to will the lasers in his head to stop. "I found a dead rabbit in the middle of the kitchen table. The liver had been cut out." She scooted closer to Weller and began running her hand slowly through his hair. His eyes began to shut. "Weller stay with me for just a few more minutes. When Minks got to your house, he looked at the liver through a portable scope. Weller, the liver was half eaten."

Weller's eyes popped all the way open as he tried to get his wits around him. "It was an old woman."

"Who was an old woman?"

"It was an old woman that speared me."

"What did she look like?" Swift got out her phone and began recording.

"Old, very old. She was bent over, and she was wearing an old gingham type dress. When she smiled, she had razor-like teeth. She stood over me when she pulled the spear out and said, "You will never save the children." I couldn't move. I couldn't speak. It was like I was paralyzed."

Swift poured ice chips in a cup and fed them slowly to Weller. Weller dozed off for a moment and then his eyes popped wide open. "She's the one killing the little girls. It has to be. I think she is eating their livers, too.

Swift's jaw dropped. "Oh my God. Those poor girls."

Weller tried to get up, but there was no energy left. "I have to stop her before she kills again."

"You couldn't stop a teddy bear right now. Go to sleep. I'll get Morris and Minks to help."

Weller's last words before he fell asleep were, "Find the old man."

Sunday, 3:00 P.M.

When Swift walked into the hospital room, the first thing she heard was Weller, "Did you find the old man?"

"Still looking. The citizens of Kenwood aren't talking. Morris contacted a Cherokee Nation Marshal. He's pretty confident he can get us close." Swift walked bedside and held Weller's hand. "How are you feeling?"

"Like I have been ridden hard and put up wet. I'll live."

"Good. Glad to hear it," Holcomb came bursting in the room. "You ready to talk yet?"

"You mind talking a little softer Holcomb. My head still feels like somebody took a hammer to it."

"Sorry about that. I get loud when I get excited. So, are you ready to answer some questions?"

"Fire away. I'm not sure I can help much though." Weller took a cup of ice off the tray and took a mouthful. Swift sat down in a vinyl hospital chair that farted every time she moved.

"What happened Saturday?"

"I came out of the bathroom. Felt something was wrong. The next thing I was laying on the floor like a stuck hog. I don't remember anything else."

Holcomb eyed Weller and then Swift. All he got was poker faces. "Alright then. I'll get back to work. If you remember anything, give me a shout." Holcomb walked out of the room.

"I don't think he believes you, Weller," A smile spread across her face as she was saying it.

"Don't really care. This will be over with very soon." Weller set his jaw and gritted through a muscle spasm in his shoulder.

"Do you need more pain meds?" Swift's chair farted as she moved. The horror on her face caused Weller to burst out laughing and then grimace in pain when his shoulder shook.

"I'm not on any pain meds. I refused them. The only thing I'm taking is Ibuprofen. Tonight you're breaking me out of this joint."

"What! No way! The doc said you were going to be in here for at least a week."

"The doc was wrong. If we wait a week, another little girl will die. Tell Morris to contact Ketcher with the Cherokee Marshal's Office. He can find out where the old man lives."

"Your wish is my command oh little one, but I don't approve. What if you break your stitches open. You could bleed out before we got you back to the hospital."

"Don't worry. I have Nurse Laura to take care of me. Here's the plan…"

Monday, 7:00 A.M.

Weller rode in Morris' personal vehicle, a 1976 Ford Expedition, to Kenwood. Swift was meeting them with the thorn-like thing Minks discovered in Grace's hair. "Pull up here Morris. We'll wait for Swift to join us.

"You got it, boss," Morris said pulling over and putting the Expedition in park.

"I'm not your boss. I wanna apologize for the way I acted at the crime scene. I lost my cool."

"Not a problem," Morris responded sitting up a little higher in the seat. "It was my bad. I should have kept everyone back."

"I also wanted to thank you for the blood you donated. I could have died without that blood.

"I guess we're blood brothers now, huh?" Morris said and then laughed at the expression on Weller's face.

"Let's don't go that far. There's Swift." Swift pulled her car off the road behind them and jumped in the back seat.

"Hey, guys. Let's go find an old man." Swift buckled her seat belt and handed an evidence bag to Weller.

"Ketcher is going to meet us at the turn-off to where the old man is living. It's only a couple of miles up here on the left, Morris."

Ketcher's patrol SUV sat at the turn off exactly where he said it was. Ketcher got out and came back to join them. "We can drive for about a half mile, and then we will have to hike a coupla' hundred yards." Ketcher was a big man, six foot three and pushing three hundred pounds. Most of it was muscle. His arms were bigger than most people's legs. You didn't want to mess with Ketcher. "Can you make it that far Weller?"

"I'll make it."

"Follow me in then. There is a place we can turn around when we are leaving." Ketcher returned to his vehicle and led off.

They drove through the undergrowth on the edge of the trees until Ketcher stopped his vehicle. Morris parked next to him. "Looks like we walk now," Weller mumbled.

"Leave your weapons here. It is considered rude to visit someone armed," Ketcher ordered as he unbuckled his service belt, and put it into a metal lock box in the back SUV.

Weller and the others locked their guns up and joined Ketcher. Weller stuffed the evidence bag in his sling and started walking. Ketcher led the way with Weller, Swift and then Morris pulling up the rear. By the time they reached the old man's shack, Weller was exhausted. Sweat rolled off his forehead like a waterfall. Using his shirt tails, he wiped the sweat away as best he could.

"Before we talk with Lone Hawk, I want you to know a few things about him. He is old, very old. He was old when my father was a boy and when his father was as well. No one knows where he came from. He has lived in this cabin for the last fifty or sixty years. No one knows where he lived before that. Some say in a cave that is under Lake Hudson now. To most people, he has always lived here. Lone Hawk does not speak English, and he believes in the old ways and traditions." Ketcher stopped to collect his thoughts. "By him allowing you to come here, he is showing respect. He knows of you and what you are trying to do."

"If there aren't any questions, let's do this." Ketcher knocked on the door and waited patiently. "I'll go in first and tell him what you want. If he is ready to talk with you, I'll get you." They heard a noise inside. Ketcher opened the door and went inside. "Osiyo Lone Hawk," is all they heard before he shut the door.

A few minutes later Ketcher opened the door and walked outside. "He will talk now, but only with Weller. There is not enough room for you two," he said pointing to Swift and Morris.

The inside of the cabin was neat with a small wood cookstove in the corner and a larger wood stove for warmth at the other end of the cabin. There were only two rooms. There was no water or electricity.

"Osiyo and thank you for talking with me." Weller said sweat still pouring from his face and forehead." Ketcher translated as Weller and Lone Hawk talked.

"Osiyo. Sit. You are injured."

Weller collapsed into a wooden dining chair. "I have many questions for you about the girls who have died recently. Do you know of these killings?" While Weller waited for Ketcher to translate, he felt blood running down his chest. The wound had reopened.

Lone Hawk walked out the back door. Weller looked at Ketcher for guidance. "I don't know. Just wait." A few minutes later he walked back in carrying what looked like a clump of mud. He took out a long knife and stepped toward Weller. Weller froze.

He cut a hole in Weller's shirt from front to back on the left side, undid the sling, and tore the bandage off his shoulder. He took the mud in his hand and placed it firmly onto the wound on both sides.

Weller grimaced as Lone Hawk pressed hard on the wound with the mud. A few moments later the blood stopped, and the pain subsided to a nuisance.

"This poultice will heal your wound. But you must keep it on for three days. After three days, take it off and wash the wound carefully."

"Thank you. It already feels better." Weller said putting the sling back over his shoulder.

"Ask your questions now. I am old, and it is time to rest."

"Three girls have been murdered in the last two months. Two more girls, missing longer than the rest, have never been found. Each girls' liver was cut out. I believe the killer is eating them. Do you have any information that can help me stop these killings?"

Lone Hawk thought for several moments before he answered. "Your people were ancient warriors from the land of the ice. The scars on your body show that you are a mighty warrior who has faced death and lived to tell about it. In the ancient days, people would sing songs about your bravery." The old man stopped. He seemed to be gathering energy to continue talking.

"Thank you for those words."

"I do not tell you this to be kind. You will need all your skills to beat this enemy."

"I don't understand. Who is this enemy?"

"The one you seek is called Spearfinger. She is of the Rock People. She is ancient, older than the trees, older than these hills. She is evil and very powerful. Stronger than three men. She eats the livers to help her feel young and energized. An ordinary man cannot defeat her. You must use your head to kill her. You are not strong enough right now to beat her. Maybe in a few weeks, but not now.

"Tell me how to defeat her."

"First you must separate her from her spear. With her spear she is deadly."

"I almost found that out first hand."

"Spearfinger is a shapeshifter. By uttering two words out loud, she can turn to any object or human. You cannot let her shapeshift, or she could simply run away and wait. She is very patient." He stopped talking so his words could sink in.

"Can you defeat her?"

"It is not for me to do. A mighty warrior must do it. I am too old. You must look deep inside yourself and come up with a plan. I can tell you where she will be and when. That is all."

"Where can I find her?" Weller was becoming more depressed the longer Lone Hawk talked.

"It is time for the gathering of nuts on Baron Fork Creek. She will be there in two days. She will not kill until then. You have until then to come up with a plan. It is time for you to go now."

"One more thing. Can you tell me what this is?" Weller

dug the evidence bag out of the sling and handed it to Grandfather.

Lone Hawk looked at it and handed it back to Weller. "It is a porcupine quill. It was used, with others, as a comb hundreds of years ago. The porcupine quill is hollow so that it gives and does not harm the head of the person using it." He pointed out the flat end. "It has been cut to fit into a wooden handle. Where did you find this?"

"We found it in the hair of the Greencorn girl."

"Spearfinger is tricking her victims by offering to comb their hair. The girls feel bound to tradition and cannot refuse her. She will find a girl off from the others and then take her into the woods."

"I am tired. Go now. Remember, only you can destroy Spearfinger."

Weller and Ketcher stepped out onto the porch and shut the door behind them. No one spoke until they got to the vehicles.

"Good luck Usdi Tsitaga Aniyvwi. You're going to need it." Ketcher said opening the lockbox and buckling on his service belt.

"People have been calling me that for the last week. What does it mean?"

Ketcher smiled. "It means Little Rooster."

Swift and Morris burst out laughing. Weller's face turned bright red. "It's not that funny."

"Yes, it is Little Rooster," Swift snorted in air as she leaned on the car laughing. Morris tried to control himself, but it was no use. He guffawed like he had heard the world's funniest joke.

"Why do they call me that Ketcher?"

"Well, the little part is easy. I'm guessing the rooster part is because you're so tough, and people say you bed a lot of women."

Swift and Morris, who had almost gotten control of themselves, literally fell to the ground howling with laughter. Weller knew he would never live this down. "I hope you two buffoons get chiggers. Let's get out of here."

Monday, 8:00 P.M.

They met that night at Weller's house. Swift and Morris brought a bucket of the Colonel's finest. Little Rooster provided the Bud Light. For the first five minutes, the buffoons laughed every time they looked at Weller. After that they settled down, they began planning. They would come up with an idea, throw it around and then out the window. Then they came up with another plan and tossed it away like out of date milk. Finally, by two in the morning, after discussing several plans and dismissing them all, they thought they had one that would work.

Wednesday, 7:00 A.M.

Already tens of families were out picking up nuts along the creek. By eight, hundreds of people would be there. Young children laughed and played together while the older children helped their parents pick up nuts. Some families would sell their nuts in Tahlequah while many others, like squirrels, would store the nuts for the winter. This year there seemed to be a bumper crop.

Weller, Swift, and Morris kept a sharp lookout for Spearfinger. So far, she was staying hidden. At supper time, the families all sat together and shared their lunches. It was a big feast for tired backs. Weller was looking down the creek when Swift's voice came over the walky-talky. "Weller, by the bridge. The little girl in the red dress. An old woman is walking toward her." Weller spotted the little girl fifty yards from the festival. She was all alone looking for crawdads. When the old woman spoke to the little girl from behind, she startled her. Weller began working his way toward the old woman who had her back turned toward him. He walked slowly, but steadily so as not to spook Spearfinger.

Meanwhile, Morris crept toward the little girl from downstream. He stopped ten feet from the little girl and waited behind an oak tree large enough to hide his bulk.

Spearfinger was so intent on the little girl that she didn't notice Weller coming up behind her. Weller got within twenty feet before he spoke, "You will not kill another little girl Spearfinger. "Without looking, Spearfinger turned and threw her spear at the same time. The spear brushed Weller's shirt as it flew by and then embedded itself in a birch trunk.

Swift had walked across the bridge and was now above Spearfinger. "Now," Weller yelled. As Swift dropped a concussion grenade off the bridge, Morris sprinted forward and pulled the little girl from harm's way. The explosion knocked Spearfinger head over heels and stole the breath from her lungs. Before she could gain her air back, Weller lassoed her shoulders and dragged her into the water. He shoved her head under the water and held it with his one good arm. Spearfinger scissor-kicked her legs trying to get Weller off of her. Knocked off balance, Weller fell to his knees and dropped his end of the rope.

Swift and Morris rushed to the creek bank and grabbed hold of the rope keeping it taut and the pressure on Spearfinger's arms.

"Keep it tight, "Weller yelled as he regained his feet in the current. Weller grabbed a new purchase of Spearfinger's hair and made a fist. He shoved her head to the bottom of the two-foot deep creek. Her legs kept kicking, but it seemed even she knew it was not worth the effort.

The Cherokees now lined the banks of the Barron Fork. Men, women, children. No word was spoken.

Weller's was tiring quickly. Even in peak shape, this would have been difficult. His shoulder throbbed and felt it when the staples in his shoulder pulled away. "I can't last much longer."

"Let us help," Swift said dropping the rope and wading into the water.

"Get back. Lone Hawk said I was the only one who could end this."

Swift backed out of the water and reached for the rope as it went limp. The struggling had stopped.

Weller released his hold. The water heated up and the clear water turned a bright green. The body melted away. He staggered up onto the bank before he collapsed.

The little girl's parents ran to her and swept her up into their arms. They sat her down and went over every inch of her body. Her cries were from fear, not pain. The people along the bank were still silent. Then as one, the walked away and began harvesting the nuts as though nothing had happened.

Morris carried Weller while Swift kept pressure on his shoulder to stem the bleeding. When they got to Morris' SUV, he placed him gently in the back and Swift crawled in after.

Weller opened his eyes briefly before Morris closed the hatch. "Morris?" It came out as a soft whisper.

"Yeah, boss?"

"Get the spear."

Morris ran like a turtle on Red Bull back to the war zone. The spear was gone. There was no mark on the tree. There was nothing on the ground.

Morris hurried back. "There's no spear boss. It's gone."

Weller sat up wiggling free of Swift.

"Lay flat Weller," Swift said trying to hold him back. "My God, how am I supposed to keep the blood in your body if you're squirming like a five- year old."

"Let go of me, Swift. Morris let the tailgate down." Morris hesitated. "Just do it, Morris."

Morris pulled up on the handle and released him. Weller jumped out and started windmilling his left arm. First forward and then backward.

"Are you crazy," Swift climbed out and stood next to Morris. Both stood silent, but their mouths were open.

"There is no more wound. It's healed. Look," Weller stripped off his bloody, water-drenched shirt and stood topless before them. "See. There's no wound. It's like it never happened."

They stood around looking at each other not knowing what to say, each trying to wrap their heads around what had happened. Finally, Morris broke the silence. "Boss, I have one questions for you. How are we going to write this up?

Three weeks later

Weller and Ketcher were back at Lone Hawk's cabin. He invited them in and motioned for them to sit. "Congratulation Little Rooster. You have defeated something that's never been beaten. I will sing of your victory for all the people to hear."

Ketcher started to translate for Weller, but Weller raised his hand and stopped him. He could understand Lone Hawk as if he were speaking English. "Thank you. Without your help, many other children would have died." When Weller spoke, it was in Cherokee. "How is it that I can understand your words now when I could not the first time

I visited you."

The old man smiled, "You must be a fast learner Little Rooster." He rose from his chair and walked a few steps over to a shelf over the bed. He returned walking backward. When he turned, he held a pipe in his hands and handed it to Weller. Ketcher watched amazed.

The old man sat back down with a grunt and smiled at Weller. "Little Rooster, I give this to you with caution. This pipe has power. Power like you have never seen before. Come closer." Weller leaned in, and Grandfather whispered to him. "In your darkest hour, you may say these two words while holding the pipe, but only when there is no other way. You must go now. I am tired"

Weller and Ketcher stood and walked toward the door. Weller stopped just before opening the door and turned around. "Will you answer one question for me?"

"What is your question Little Rooster?"

"Are you of the Dogwood People?" Weller found that he no longer minded his nickname. He was proud of it. Lone Hawk smiled. He thought for a moment before he spoke. "The answer is in your heart Little Rooster."

Weller and Swift sat on his front porch drinking a Bud Light and rocking. Weller had just told her of his meeting with the old man, everything but about the pipe. He was still unsure about that part.

The sun was starting to fade in the west, which began a cricket symphony in the yard. Swift was the first to break the silence. "I've been wondering and a little worried about two things."

"Shoot."

"It's three weeks now since we closed the case. You haven't tried to get me in bed yet. Why is that?"

"Weller's don't beg." a grin so big it almost touched his

ears spread across his face.

Swift punched him in the arm spilling a little of his beer. She turned away from him and pretended to pout.

"That was one thing, what is the other?"

"Well I have been studying Cherokee online," Swift turned back toward him. "This case got me interested. You know how some words can mean two things sometimes."

"Yes?"

"What if instead of 'Little Rooster' those words translate into 'Little Cock!" Swift jumped up, raced through the front door, and to the bedroom. Weller was close behind.

9. MORE THAN ONE MISSING

By JOHN D KETCHER JR

10 p.m. Friday

The West Side Tavern parking lot was full of vehicles when a dark colored 1996 Buick pulled in and parked on the back row. A glow illuminated the interior of the car as the driver struck a match lighting up a cigarette. "The wait begins. The hunt is on. It won't be long now," the driver said to himself. Scanning the area, he noticed the only lighting for the parking lot was directly in front. *Good.*

Smoke still lingered in the air from his second cigarette when a woman staggered out of the bar and headed to her car. Look at the body on that woman; sexy, slender and large breasts. Moreover, she was right in front of his car. Snuffing the smoke out, the man eased out of his car and quietly walked up behind her. He covered the woman's mouth with his hand and dragged her to his car.

When the woman realized what was happening she fought like a hellcat: biting, kicking and hitting him all over his body. The man spun the woman around. His closed fist connected with her cheekbone with a crunch and knocked the fight out of her as she crumpled in his arms.

The man looked around to see if anyone noticed, but they were alone. Opening the trunk lid the kidnapper pulled out the duct tape and secured her mouth, hands, and feet. He pushed her into the hideaway compartment in the trunk. The man replaced the paneling and exited the parking lot heading north on Maple Street. A pair of black loafers lying on the gravel parking lot was the only evidence of her kidnapping.

11 p.m. Friday

Backing into his garage the man stopped two feet from the door leading to his special room. Unlocking the door to his room he turned the lights on and surveyed the room making sure everything was ready. Walls and floor covered with new plastic? Check. Knives on the workbench located the north wall? Check. The refrigerator filled with food and drink? Check. Clean towels in the bathroom after he finished working? Check.

Good. The man thought. *Time to go to work.* He returned to the car and carried the unconscious woman inside the room and locked the door.

Suzy attempted to move her arms and legs but she couldn't. *Why can't I move?* She looked up and realized her arms were above her head and chained to a large u-hook in the ceiling, leaving her bare legs dangling several inches above the floor.

Suzy tried to remember what happened. *Where am I? How did I get here?* Closing her eyes, she focused on the last thing she remembered. *I staggered out of the West Side Tavern in P. Creek and headed to my car then...then I can't remember what happened after that. Where are my clothes* she thought to herself as she realized she was naked.

"Help me! Someone help me!" She yelled while jerking at the chains.

"No one can hear you," said a soft voice from behind her. "The room is soundproof."

Suzy stiffened at the sound of the voice. A cold fear swept over her that this wasn't a bad dream, but a living nightmare. "This can't be happening to me. Please let me go! I won't tell anyone. I promise. I promise," she pleaded.

"That's what the others said. Do they ever keep their word? No, they don't."

"There were others? What happened to them?"
Silence.
"What happened to them?"
"Tell me, Suzy Bales, what would you do to stay alive?"
"How do you know my name?" Came a frightened reply.
"I have your driver's license. You were born on 13 May 1998. Umm. That makes you 20 years old. Height: 60 inches. Weight: 100 pounds. Shall I go on?"
"No."
"Good. Let's play some music. How about country music?" He tuned the radio into a country station just as Loretta Lynn belted out, "I want a man with a slow hand."

"No, No." She yelled as the man's fingers went down her neck to her buttocks. Suzy closed her eyes and tried to pull away as he moved around to her front. The man continued tracing around her breasts several times then down to her love box. When she jerked away, he grabbed her ass with his left hand and with his other hand roughly shoved his middle finger in and out.

"Stop it! You bastard." She yelled as she kicked at him.
Teasingly the man said, "Suzy."
Suzy opened her eyes and saw a tall man with a beer gut,

buck naked and not a single hair on his body. "What are you going to do?"

Suzy screamed again as the man moved in closer.

1 p.m. Sunday

A middle-aged lady opened the door leading into the Chouteau Police Station. Unsure of what to do she hesitated before she entered any farther. Seeing a dispatcher behind her desk, she walked over to her.

"How may I help you?" asked Sheila Irwin.

"I am Edna Bales. My daughter is missing. I'm worried something has happened to her." She blurted out as tears flowed down her face. Sheila placed a box of Kleenex near the edge of her desk.

"Just a minute Mrs. Bales." Sheila said, "Officer Davis, a Mrs. Bales to see you."

"Please have a seat, Mrs. Bales," Officer Davis pointed to a chair next to his desk.

"Thank you."

"How may I help you?"

"As I told the young lady, my daughter is missing. I'm worried she's in trouble." A watershed of tears flowed down Mrs. Bales' face.

"How old is she and when did you last see her?"

"She's 20. We had supper together 5 p.m. Friday evening at Pop's & Gigi's. She was going out with some friends to a party."

"Are you sure she's not just staying with some friends?"

"I've tried calling and texting, but she's not answering. I've called her friends, but they haven't seen her since Friday night. Officer, she's not like that. She always calls or texts me if she's going to stay overnight someplace. We always go to church on Sunday and then we go to lunch.

I'm afraid something has happened. Maybe she's been in a wreck and needs help."

"I understand Mrs. Bales. Now please fill out this information sheet. Put down when and where you last saw your daughter. I will need the names and phone numbers of her friends. Tell me her full name and what kind of car does she drive." Officer Davis said

"Suzy Bales. That's Suzy with a ZY. She drives a silver 2015 Toyota Camry. Is there anything I can do?" as she filled out the form.

"You could have flyers made and post them around town. Maybe some of Suzy's friends can help you. In the meantime, I'll contact P. Creek police and Mayes County Sheriff to be on the lookout."

Mrs. Bales looked down at her purse in an attempt to regain her composure before leaving. She stood up, thanked the officer for his help and headed home.

9 p.m. Sunday

"David Myers, its 9 p.m., where are you going?" Asked his mother, Mary Beth Myers. "You haven't spent any time with me in a long time."

"I'm going out, mom."

"It would be nice to spend a little time with you," she repeated. "I don't have too many friends left in this world. I get lonesome sometimes." The sadness and desperation could be heard in her voice as she spoke.

David took a seat next to his mom and put his arm around her and said, "Tell you what. Let's go someplace for lunch tomorrow. You choose the place. Okay?"

"I would like to go to Pop's & Gigi's in Chouteau. Would that be okay?"

"It'll be fine. We'll get there at 11 am before the lunch

crowd arrives. Don't wait up. I'll see you in the morning. Night, mom."

Nag. Nag. Nag. David thought. *That's all she ever does. Why doesn't mom go to bed like other little old people? She should be thankful I'm providing a roof over her head and food on the table. One day, maybe, one day.*

10 a.m. Monday

"Chouteau Police. How may I help you?" answered Officer Davis.

"Officer Davis, this is Detective Isaac Tic-ah-nee-skee from P. Creek Police. We've found your missing car. The owner of the West Side Tavern had it towed away Saturday morning. There are a couple of items I want to verify with you. How long has the young lady been missing?"

"Since Friday evening according to her mother."

"And the clothing she was wearing?"

"Let me check the report. Oh, yes here it is. White short-sleeve blouse, black slacks, and black loafers. What happens now?"

"I'm going to have a look around the parking lot at West Side Tavern and then at Miss Bales car. I'll let you know what I find."

Detective Tic-ah-nee-skee grabbed his notebook and jotted down a few notes. He made two phone calls one to Detective Weller and another to the owner of the West Side Tavern.

He called the Mayes County Sheriff's Office and asked for Detective Weller.

"Hey, Tic, how's things going in your neck of the woods?"

"O, fair to partly middling today. I'm looking for some county stats on missing people over the last ten years."

"What's up?"

"Have a missing person report, and something doesn't feel right."

"Would that be Suzy Bales reported missing by her mother?"

"That's the one."

"I'll get it together in the next day or two. Will give you a call when I have everything."

"Later."

Next, he called the owner of the West Side Tavern. "Phil, Tic-ah-nee-skee here. I'm heading your way. Need you to show me where that car you had towed was parked." Tic-ah-nee-skee headed out.

Phil was waiting outside when Tic-ah-nee-skee drove up.

"Hey, Tic-ah-nee-skee. How's your son?"

"Fine and how's wife?"

"Don't know and don't care. My wife left me for one of my customers. If he ever comes back, I'll give him free beer for a year." Phil said. Seeing the confused look on Tic-ah-nee-skee's face, he grinned. "Prenup. Says if she screws around she gets nothing. That man just saved me from having to sell my business. Isn't life great! Over here is where the car was parked."

Tic-ah-nee-skee looked the area over but found nothing unusual. "Three days would have covered up any tracks." He said to no one in particular. Scanning over the gravel parking lot he spied something lying on the ground about 50 feet away. He stopped when he saw two black loafers. He called the office. "I've found the crime scene of the missing young lady. Have Miss Bales' car towed to our back lot."

11 a.m. Monday

David opened the door for his mom as they entered Pop's & Gigi's.

"Thank you, David. The cafe is such a nice place. Oh, look there's a poster of a young girl who's missing. She's such a lovely girl. I bet her mother is worried. I know I would be."

"Yes, she was a lovely girl."

"What was that?"

"I said she's a lovely girl. I hope they find her."

"Welcome to Pop's & Gigi's. Seating for two?" asked the waitress with bright red hair.

"Yes. Mom, where would you like to sit?" David asked as he eyed the waitress. One day.

"A booth please."

"Follow me please." She led them to a booth with a scenic view of truckers speeding by on Highway 69.

"My name is Rita, and I'll be your waitress. What would you like to drink?"

"I noticed the poster of the missing girl. Do you know her?" Mary Beth asked.

"Yes, we grew up together here in Chouteau. We're all worried about Suzy," Rita pointed to a booth across from them saying "That's Suzy's mother. Mrs. Bales. She's just worried sick."

"I'll have water and coffee, please," Mary Beth said as she went to talk with Mrs. Bales.

"Just coffee for me," Replied David. Watching his mom, he smiled thinking about the irony of watching the mother of the kidnapped young woman talking to the mother of the son who kidnapped the young woman.

The café door opened and David turned his head to see who entered. He saw two men come and froze. Hatred bubbled up from deep inside his bones as his eyes bored in on Detective Isaac Tic-ah-nee-skee. *What's that son-of-a-bitch doing here?* He thought. David quickly recovered and looked away but not before the detective saw him and smiled.

Rita seated the two men in the back room. "What would you boys like to drink?"

"Coke for me," Ben answered.

"Coffee will be fine."

"I'll be right back with your drinks then I'll take your order," Rita said.

"Okay, dad. I saw the look that man gave you. What's his beef with you?"

"Mr. Myers was a person of interest, a missing person investigation. It appears he hasn't forgiven me for hauling him in."

9 p.m. Monday

Suzy, still hanging from the ceiling, woke up with a start when she heard the door open. David carried in a body over his shoulder and dropped it on the ground. It was a young man about her age with dark hair and medium built. She watched David chain the man's wrists and attach a cable to the chain. *What is he doing* she thought?

David hoisted the young man up using a pulley system he had rigged making it easier to hang an unconscious person from the ceiling. He placed an eight-foot step ladder underneath the pulley system, climbed up and lifted the chain off the pulley over onto the ceiling hook. Next, he cut off the man's shirt, trousers, and underwear. The shoes and socks came off last leaving the young man naked. David grabbed the clothing and threw them into the trash can over in the corner.

That's what he did to me Suzy thought as a shudder flowed through her body.

"Lucy! I'm home!" David said.

192

"My name's not Lucy." Suzy angrily responded.

"What? You never watched 'I Love Lucy'? When her husband, Ricky, walked through the front door and said 'Lucy! I'm home!'"

Suzy refused to answer him."

"Not talking? Too bad. Still, I got you a new roommate. Thought you two could hang around together for a while." Laughing at his humor David continued. "Let me introduce you two. Suzy this is Ben. Ben? Oh, wait he's still unconscious."

David walked to a table along the back wall and grabbed a rubber hose three foot long. He beat the young man and yelled "Wake up! Wake up!" Each swing of the hose was harder than the last. Slap. Slap. Slap.

He kept swinging until Suzy screamed, "Stop it, you're hurting him!"

"Keep your mouth shut while I'm working," David said as he turned his attention to Suzy. Whack! Whack! Whack! She screamed for him to stop but he continued beating her unmercifully.

"Now look at what you've done. You know what this means?" David said with an evil grin on his face. She screamed again as he took off his trousers.

11 p.m. Monday

Office Ricky Howard was answering a disturbance call in the 400 block of SE 5th street when he came upon a husband and wife fighting on the front lawn. Seeing the flashing lights of the patrol car the couple stood up. Davis almost lost his composure at seeing a fat old man in his underwear and a fat old woman in her nightgown rolling on the ground.

Walking over to the couple Officer Howard asked, "Are

you two fighting or trying to have sex on your front lawn?" The old couple looked at him as if the officer was crazy. Howard told them if they're fighting he would let them go back inside with a warning. However, if they were trying to have sex in public, he would take them to jail. Howard pointed down, and the old man realized he had become aroused.

Embarrassed he stuttered "We…we were fighting."

"Then I suggest you two take it back inside." Howard said, "And no more fighting."

The old man started to respond when his wife grabbed him by the arm and led him away. "Old man, let's get back into the house and continue this conversation," She said.

Oh, God. I'm not going to be able to get rid of those images for as long as I live Howard thought. Passing by the Sertoma Senior Citizens Center on S. Rowe Street he wondered if the old couple ate lunch there on Friday's. *Come on, Howard quit thinking about them.*

Turning left on SE 3rd Street he noticed a silver 2015 Toyota Camry parked in one of the car wash stalls. When he pulled in behind the car he spotted the spray handle lying on the ground. Opening the car, he saw the keys still in the ignition. Howard called in the tag number. Dispatch called back with the name of the owner. "Oh, crap. You'd better call Detective Tic-ah-nee-skee. I'll wait here."

Isaac Tic-ah-nee-skee was settled in his favorite lounge chair reading *Nowhere to Run,* by C. J. Box. He was getting into the part where the Wyoming game warden was getting his butt kicked by two poachers when his phone rang. "Detective Tic-ah-nee-skee."

"This is dispatch, Debra Smarr. Officer Howard found your son's car at the car wash east of Thomas Restaurant. Keys are still in the car. Is your son with you?"

"No. Tell Officer Howard to tape off the crime area. I'm

headed there now."

1 a.m. Tuesday

David stepped back to admire his handy work. Blood dripped from his knife. Suzy's body jerked side to side from the horrific torture David had inflicted on her.

Suzy cried, her voice too hoarse and croaky from all the screaming. He watched the blood drip from her body onto the plastic covered floor. The cuts were not deep enough to cause death, but just below the skin to cause bleeding and pain.

"Hey, Ben. What do you think?"

Ben struggled to turn his body. Seeing the bloody mess, he yelled "You sick bastard. One day you'll get…" David slammed his fist into Ben's stomach.

"Shut up!" David screamed. "You and your dad think you're better than us." *Thump*, another hit to the midriff. "Your dad harassing my family and me for years." *Thump*! *Thump*! "Accusing me of kidnapping without proof." *Thump*! *Thump*! "Accusing my father of kidnapping without proof." *Thump*! *Thump*!

"It's payback time." Holding up the bloody knife he used on Suzy, David placed the knifepoint just above Ben's right nipple and sliced downward leaving a quarter inch deep cut all the way to his waist. Ben clamped his teeth together to keep from screaming as cut after cut ripped down his body. Completing the downward cuts, David sliced across Ben's chest from left to right from the shoulders down to the hips creating a crosshatching pattern.

"Now for the backside," David whispered as he traced the knifepoint from the left nipple around to Ben's backside. Ben passed out.

2 a.m. Tuesday

Detective Tic-ah-nee-skee had Ben's car towed to the police station and placed an APB out on his son.

"Officer Howard, there's nothing more we can do here," Tic-ah-nee-skee said. "I'll be in my office looking at old files for possible suspects."

"Yes, sir."

Sitting in his car outside the police station Tic-ah-nee-skee, the father, broke down and cried. *Not my son, too. First, my wife goes missing and now my son. Why God? Why? Please help me.* Regaining his composure, the father transformed back into Tic-ah-nee-skee the detective and did what he does best. Find evidence and put bad guys in jail.

Detective Tic-ah-nee-skee entered the building and waved at Debra as she buzzed the security door in the lobby open. He walked briskly down the hallway to his office. Tic-ah-nee-skee took off his coat Tic-ah-nee-skee rolled up his sleeves and dug into thirty-five years of old cases.

6:30 a.m. Tuesday

David finished with his shower and dressed in clean clothes before stepping out of the bathroom in front of Suzy and Ben.

"Well, what do you think?" David asked. "Can't find the words to describe me, huh? You're too kind."

Taking his time David walked around eyeing them like a rancher would size up his prize stallion and mare.

"I have to leave you now for a little while. I'm preparing breakfast and coffee for my mom. However, don't worry. I'll be back soon and we'll finish what we started and then

196

take a little trip to my property," David said as he locked the door on his way out.

"Suzy, we have to get out of here, or we're going to die," Ben said.

"How? We're chained up?"

"Since I was a small boy my dad told me never give up. Always give it your all. We can do this." Ben started swinging his feet frontward and back gaining momentum, and with each backward motion he was able to propel himself forward, and he was able to catch the chain a little higher up.

"You can do it, Ben. Don't give up," Suzy gasped.

Ben realized his strength was fading and only had one or two more swings left in him. Just as he felt the slack in the chain, he whipped the chain up over the u-hook and fell to the floor with a thump.

"Ben, get up! Please, get up!" Suzy yelled.

Struggling to his knees, Ben crawled over to the little refrigerator and took out a bottle of water. Opening it, he drank a long swig and poured the rest over his head. His strength returning Ben grabbed another bottle and pulled the step ladder over to Suzy. Climbing up to Suzy he gave her some water "I'm going to move the ladder in front of you and help you down. Ready?"

Ben repositioned the ladder in front of her. He stepped up behind her and said, "Suzy put your feet on the steps. Good. I'm here for you. Now take one step up. That's it. I'm going to reach up and unhook you," Ben reached up and unhooked the chain. "Done. Let's go down one step at a time."

Reaching the floor, they collapsed not moving for several minutes.

Finally, Ben moved over to the refrigerator again and took out two more bottles of water. Before closing the door, he spied two chocolate bars and grabbed them. "Here, we need to eat the chocolate bars for energy to do what we have to do to survive. Let's get over by the door and get ready for when he returns," Ben said to Suzy.

They helped each other up and leaned on the table to move closer to the wall. Sliding along the table Suzy grabbed a knife from the rack and hobbled to the wall.

6:45 a.m. Tuesday

Frustrated at the lack of headway in finding his son Tic-ah-nee-skee stood up and stretched. He grabbed his coffee cup and headed to the dispatch room for coffee.

"Any leads?" Debra asked.

"None," Tic-ah-nee-skee said as he filled his cup. "Something nagging me. It comes to the surface, and when I try to grab hold, it sinks back into the abyss."

"I find when trying to remember something, I shift my focus onto something else and it comes to me. Like where did you and your son eat lunch yesterday?"

"We had lunch at Pop's & Gigi's and…That's it. Thanks, Debra." Tic-ah-nee-skee rushed to his office.

Determination renewed, Tic-ah-nee-skee searched through his files and found the case on a young woman in 1983. His first missing person case. Flipping through the pages, he saw the name of a person of interest: Terry Myers. Address 600 Maple Street. Dropping the folder, he searches through the files for a missing person in 2013. Here it is, a person of interest: David Myers. Address 600 Maple Street. Tic-ah-nee-skee hot-tailed it to his car.

7 a.m. Tuesday

"Oh, David. Thank you for the wonderful breakfast and

coffee," His mother said.

"You're welcome, mom. It was a nice time. I'll be heading out in a little bit. Going to Adair to bid on a couple of construction jobs. Probably be gone all day," David said as he drank the last of his coffee. He put the dishes in the sink and kissed his mom on the top of her head as he left.

Turning the keys to his special room David hesitated. *Something doesn't feel right.* David glanced around and saw nothing out of place. *Nerves* he thought. Shaking his head, he opened the door and entered the room.

"He's turning the lock to the door. Get ready," Ben whispered to Suzy.

Ben stands and draws back his arms with the chain dangling from his hands. David steps into the room as Ben swings the chain as hard as he can into David's face. Suzy hits David's left kneecap with her chain. Both keep hitting David as he fell to the ground screaming. They knew if David got up they were dead.

Suzy climbed on top of David's legs and sliced through his trousers and underwear. She grabbed his penis and stretched it out and placed the knife at the base. "You'll never rape another woman again!" She yelled as she sliced his penis off and handed it to him. David watched in horror as blood flowed from his groin and horrific pain doubled him over into a fetal position.

"What's all that noise out here?" Mrs. Myers asked. Seeing two naked and bloodied people she screamed and retreated into her house. Locking the door, she dialed 911. Ben and Suzy staggered outside.

7:05 a.m. Tuesday

Tic-ah-nee-skee was pulling in the driveway of David Myers house when he saw two naked and bloodied people stagger outside the garage. He picked up the radio and said "Officer needs assistance at 600 N. Maple Street. Send two ambulances."

Dropping the mic, he headed to the two victims. Recognizing Ben, he ran to him, but Ben stopped him. "Dad, we're cut up bad and in pain. Could you get us a couple of blankets?"

Tic-ah-nee-skee retrieved two blankets from his car and gently placed them around Suzy and Ben. Then the father mode kicked in, and Tic-ah-nee-skee wrapped one arm around his son and cried. Leaning over Ben whispered, "I didn't give up, dad." They both cried.

Sirens could be heard coming down Maple Street.

"Dad, I want you to meet Suzy Bales. Suzy this is my dad, Detective Isaac Tic-ah-nee-skee."

"Glad to make your acquaintance. Now if you'll excuse me I'm going to tell your mother we found you." Tic-ah-nee-skee stood up and walked into the street to direct the incoming law enforcement as he made a call to tell Officer Davis the good news.

7:25 a.m. Tuesday

Life flight transported Dave Myers to Tulsa with life-threatening injuries. The flight nurse told Tic-ah-nee-skee that Myers had a 15 percent chance of surviving.

Suzy and Ben were checked out by the emergency medical personnel and taken to Mayes County Hospital. Tic-ah-nee-skee promised he'd be there soon.

Officer Howard walked up and said, "Detective Tic-ah-nee-skee, Officer Williams needs you inside."

Tic-ah-nee-skee nodded and said, "Lead the way."

Stepping inside the doorway Tic-ah-nee-skee looked on in disbelief at the amount of blood on the floor and walls.

"Have you taken pictures of everything? Collected evidence?"

"Yes. Just like you taught us. However, there's something you need to see over in the corner." Officer Williams said as he led the way to a cork board and a four-drawer desk.

"On the cork board are 50 driver's licenses. The oldest is dated 1955, and newest is Miss Bales. Then look at this." Williams opened a desk drawer filled with purses, mementos, and driver's licenses. "The other three drawers are like this one. David Myers wasn't born until 1964. Think the father started killing and passed it on to his son?"

Tic-ah-nee-skee's focus was on the cork board. The detective took a glove out of his pocket and pulled a license off and looked at it. Williams noticed Tic-ah-nee-skee's face turn white before he collapsed on the desk crying. Soon Tic-ah-nee-skee regained his composure stood up and turned to leave. "Officer Williams, take over. Tell the Chief there's more than one missing. Call Detective Weller at MCSO and OSBI to inform them what we found. I'm going to be with my son."

"What happened?" Officer Howard asked Williams as Tic-ah-nee-skee headed out the door.

Officer Williams picked up the driver's license, Tic-ah-nee-skee had dropped. He read the name on it, Mary Tic-ah-nee-skee. "Detective Tic-ah-nee-skee just found out what happened to his missing wife."

ABOUT THE AUTHORS

Paul G. Buckner is an award-winning author, a Cherokee Nation citizen, musician, and an avid outdoorsman. He attended Northeastern State University and holds a bachelor's degree in Business Management and a Masters of Business Administration. He lives in Claremore, Oklahoma with his wife Jody and son Chase.

Mark Cook, creator of Last Wednesday Writers, is a member of the Cherokee Nation and holds a bachelor's degree in journalism from Northeastern State University. Mark has taught English for fifteen years at an at-risk high school and has taught photography to adults for ten years. He is married to his wife Lisa and they enjoy their four dogs together in Pryor, Oklahoma.

Aarika Copeland is the author of several short stories published through various online media. She has three children, whom she affectionately refers to as fire-breathing dragons. She is married to her high school sweetheart Jon, and enjoys reading and writing when she's not battling cute and ferocious dragons. She lives in Claremore, Oklahoma.

Julie Jones is a contributor to many freelance blogs, which she has enjoyed for the last few years. She too lives in Claremore with her husband of sixteen years, Steve, and their two children. She enjoys reading, writing, the outdoors, and painting.

John D Ketcher Jr is a Cherokee Nation citizen, a retired U.S. Marine Gunnery Sergeant and a retired UMC minister having earned a Masters in Divinity at St. Paul's School of Theology in Kansas City, Mo. He has been married to his wife, Paula Ruth, for the last thirty-eight years. Together they have four sons, eight grandchildren and one great grandchild. He enjoys reading and woodcarving, and lives in Pryor, Oklahoma.

www.ingramcontent.com/pod-product-compliance
Lightning Source LLC
Chambersburg PA
CBHW071907220626
47052CB00002B/250